Volleyballs, Vanilla Crème, and Vendettas

NOLA ROBERTSON

ISBN: 978-1-953213-40-2

Also by Nola Robertson

A Cumberpatch Cove Mystery

Death and Doubloons
Sabers, Sails, and Murder
Cauldrons and Corpses
Pets, Paws, and Poisons
Paints and Poltergeists
Crimes and Crystal Balls

Hawkins Harbor Cozy Mystery

Lattes and Larceny (Prequel)
Bodies, Brews, and Beaches
Volleyballs, Vanilla Crème, and Vendettas

CHAPTER ONE

The mid-morning sun warmed my skin the instant I stepped out onto the back porch of The Flavored Bean, the beachside coffee shop where I worked. Other than a few white clouds sparsely dotting the pale blue sky in the distance, the weather promised a day of sunshine without rain. I couldn't see the ocean from where I was standing, but I could smell the brine and feel the humidity in the air.

I scanned the area, searching for signs of movement in the form of a yellowish-orange-and-white-striped tabby. "Quincy, here, kitty, kitty," I called, then made smacking noises with my lips. I shook the plastic cup filled with miniature fish-shaped morsels that I'd gotten from a container I kept inside.

Quincy was a stray cat who lived near the beach and occasionally showed up to torment Harley, the lovable Havanese dog I'd recently adopted. Unlike the tentative relationship the two animals shared, which involved barking and chasing, the one between the cat and me was based on slowly developing trust. Of course, bribing him with cat food every day had definitely helped with the progress I was making.

After a few more shakes, I heard a meow and rustling

in the four-foot shrubs filling the plant bed next to the building. Quincy stretched as he emerged from his napping spot beneath the lower branches.

"Hey, Quincy," I cooed. "Would you like a snack?"

He sat in the dirt about ten feet away and eyed me expectantly but refused to come any closer. This had gotten to be his regular routine for the last few days. I knew he'd take off running if I stepped off the porch. "This food isn't free. You're going to have to let me pet you eventually." I'd done some online research and knew, with a lot of patience, it was possible to befriend stray cats.

I found his meows adorable even though they bordered on pitiful. I was convinced that all four-legged critters of the domestic variety were pros at begging. "Okay." I sighed. "Here you go." I poured some morsels into one of the two pet bowls I kept on the edge of the porch and added fresh water to the other.

The first time Quincy and I'd met, he'd been hiding under the shop's deck. Our introduction began with me being startled and ended with me landing on my backside in the dirt. It was also when I'd found Harley and decided to give him a home. I'd do the same for the cat if he let me. For now, I'd have to be content with ensuring the poor thing stayed nourished.

I walked back into the shop and took a moment to inhale and enjoy the combined smells of brewed coffees and freshly baked scones and muffins. Having a management role in an environment filled with tantalizing aromas was definitely a perk. A day on my feet might be exhausting, but it was nowhere near as stressful as the big city office job I'd left behind. Something I'd appreciated every day since I'd arrived in Hawkins Harbor, a town located on the Florida coast.

The morning rush was over. The only people remaining were sitting at a couple of the tables and occupying two seats at the counter running along the back wall. I glanced through the glass doors offering a view of the deck and the tan-colored sandy beach beyond. The umbrella-covered tables outside had also been vacated.

"How did it go with Quincy?" Archer asked as soon as I entered the room. My boss, the Bean's owner, was sitting on the end seat at the customer counter, sipping a large cup of coffee. He'd lived in town his entire life, which, if going by his appearance, had been quite a few years. The silver strands in his short haircut dominated the dark ones. The deep tan on his face and arms resulted from the time he'd spent on his boat.

I couldn't tell by his amused grin if he was genuinely interested or if he thought I was wasting my time trying to befriend a stray animal. "I think I'm making headway," I said, joining Zoey, my co-worker and friend, in the prep area. "He actually comes when I call him now. Though he still won't get close enough to let me pet him."

Zoey was busy preparing an order. Her hair was gathered in a tie at the back of her head, her crimson curls bouncing as she worked. The only uniform we were required to wear was a full-length brown apron with handy pockets below the waist. Since I no longer had to deal with dry-cleaning bills, I could wear shorts of a decent length instead of pants whenever I wanted to, which, because of the warm weather, was frequent.

"You've done wonders with Harley," Zoey said, the sparkle in her green eyes matching the beaming smile she shot me over her shoulder. "I have no doubt you'll befriend Quincy in no time."

Her fondness for any creature who happened to enter her world included giving them all names. She'd even named all the brightly colored fish in the large aquarium built into the wall behind the customer counter. Though she'd told me what they were as she'd pointed them out individually, I couldn't remember most of them.

"I appreciate the support, but I think Quincy is going to be a lot tougher to charm than Harley was," I said. Because of my dog's friendly nature and how easily he took to being on a leash, Archer thought he might have belonged to someone who'd abandoned him. Based on that assumption, I'd diligently tried to find his previous owner. After several weeks without any responses to my newspaper postings and word of mouth, I decided to keep him.

Zoey chuckled as she snapped the lid on a to-go cup, then handed it to the man waiting near the order section of the serving counter. "There you go."

"Thanks, Zoey," he said and headed for the door.

"You're still going to the game this afternoon, right?" Zoey asked me.

"I wouldn't miss it for anything," I said, knowing how important the event was to Zoey. I'd never been much of a sports fan, but hanging out on the beach and watching a live volleyball game sounded fun.

It also felt good knowing the tickets my friends and I'd purchased would be helping out a good cause. This year's event was donating their proceeds to the children's section of the local hospital. The annual tournament consisted of two co-ed teams of local volunteers. One team was called the Sarsaparilla Seagulls, and the other was the Frappuccino Flounders. Whoever came up with the names had a good sense of humor or quite the imagination. Maybe even both.

Zoey was assigned to the Seagulls and had practiced almost every night after work for the last several weeks. When she'd first told me about the games, I wasn't sure if she'd been afraid I wouldn't attend. She'd quickly pointed out that some of the guys would be flashing rippling muscles. I might not be searching for dating prospects, but I wouldn't pass on an opportunity to watch some good-looking guys in action, so hearing the latter had been another incentive to attend.

In the short time I'd lived here, Zoey had become a good friend. She'd made me feel welcome from the moment I met her and had done her best to help me transition into my new position at the Bean. I would've supported her even if she'd told me she would be wrestling alligators.

I didn't know if an age range had been set for the players or if anyone could play. The locals came in all ages, but because of The Pelican Promenade Retirement Community, many of the residents were retirees, including my aunt's friends Myrna and Vincent.

The beach, marina, and town's wide selection of shopping always guaranteed an influx of visiting tourists, so the organization sponsoring the event expected a good turnout.

The front door opened, and Delia stepped inside, flashing everyone a smile. My aunt met with her friends for breakfast most mornings. They'd already come and gone. She hadn't said anything about coming back, so I was surprised to see her again. Concerned that something bad had happened, I hurried around the counter and asked, "Is everything all right?"

"Everything's fine." Delia stepped aside to let another woman enter. "I wanted to introduce you to Melanie Merrick."

I wiped my hand on my apron before holding it out. "It's nice to meet you."

"Brinley, right?" Melanie asked, taking my hand.

"Uh-huh," I said. Before I moved to town, Delia had told all her friends and acquaintances about me. It was still a little unnerving to have people I'd never met treat me as if they already knew me.

"Delia's helping me collect the items for our raffle table," Melanie said. I must've appeared confused because she added, "For the volleyball tournament."

"Yes, of course," I said, remembering my aunt had mentioned her plans to help the non-profit organization if they needed additional volunteers.

Melanie had to be busy with the games scheduled for that afternoon, and I didn't think their visit was entirely social. "Are we donating something?" I glanced at Archer since he hadn't said anything to me about participating in the raffle.

"We are," he said, taking a sip from his cup, then placing it on the counter as he pushed off his seat. "Let me get it for you." He disappeared into the back of the building where the kitchen, storage room, office, and bathrooms were located.

Archer returned a few minutes later carrying a good-sized basket sealed with cellophane and topped with an artfully designed dark blue bow. He must've kept the basket in the storeroom because I hadn't seen it when I was in the office earlier.

I widened my eyes. "Wow. I didn't know you enjoyed doing crafts." Archer rarely blushed, but my teasing brought additional color to his cheeks.

"I don't." He snorted as he set the basket on the counter. "I take all the contents to Sadie Wooster at Unusual Trinkets, and she puts it together for me."

Maybe I'd imagined it, but Archer's eyes lit up when he mentioned Sadie's name. He wasn't married and didn't have a girlfriend. At least not one that he'd mentioned. If Sadie was one of our customers, I didn't know her by name and wasn't familiar with her business. "I don't think I've been to her place yet," I said.

"It's a cute little gift store on the other side of town," Delia said. "I'll take you the next time we go shopping."

The basket was beautifully handcrafted, and I couldn't resist slowly turning it in a circle to see all the contents. There were colorful bags of different flavored coffees, two mugs with our shop's logo, some gift cards (also for the shop), and clear plastic packages of coffee-flavored candy.

Since we didn't sell candy, I assumed Archer had purchased them from Dreamy Delectables. The store was one of my favorite places to shop and carried the largest assortment of sweets I'd ever seen.

"We always get compliments on Archer's baskets,"

Melanie said. "And a lot of ticket purchases."

"Well, she did a great job," I said.

"I think so, too," Zoey said. "If I didn't already work here, I'd try my luck at winning this basket."

Out of habit, I glanced outside, expecting to see my dog tethered to the railing, and got concerned when I didn't see him. Delia lived in a neighborhood near the beach and didn't have a fenced-in yard, so she always brought him with her when she visited the shop. "Did you leave Harley at home?"

Besides taunting me, Luna, my aunt's temperamental Persian cat, also loved to torment Harley. Delia had a lot of nice things in her home, and I always worried something might get broken if the two animals were left alone without supervision.

"Myrna took him for a walk in the park," Delia said.

The way Myrna doted on her pet guinea pig, Ziggy, I knew she'd take good care of my dog. The woman had more pictures of her precious little critter on her cell phone than most parents had of their children.

"She'll meet us at the game later, which reminds me." Delia reached into her purse, pulled out a ticket, and handed it to me. "I need to do some grocery shopping when I finish helping Melanie, and I might not be home when you stop by to change."

"Is Vincent going to be there?" I asked. He hadn't said anything when they were in for breakfast, but I'd assumed he'd be attending since the three of them liked to hang out at local events together.

"Yes," Delia said. "He and Myrna plan to get there early so they can save seats and watch everyone warm up."

"Great," I said. "Is there anything you need me to grab from the house?"

"Only what you think you'll need," Delia said. "My things are already in the car."

"We still have a couple more stops, so we need to get going," Melanie said, a hint of impatience in her tone.

"Thanks again for the donation." She grabbed the basket off the counter and urged Delia toward the door.

CHAPTER TWO

The scattered palm trees growing near the beach didn't offer much shade. I'd brought a large bottle of sunscreen, a pair of dark-lensed sunglasses, and a white floppy hat with the words "Hawkins Harbor" printed in black along the brim.

The game started late in the afternoon, so the locals with day jobs could take off early to attend or play if they were on one of the teams. It wasn't a problem for me since the Bean wasn't open all day, and Archer insisted on doing the closing chores for Zoey and me.

The area where the sidewalk bordered the beach was roped off with colorful pennant flags, which only stood a few feet off the ground. Stepping over the rope and slipping through the crowds without paying would be easy. Teenagers would be the ones most likely to sneak inside. I didn't see any security personnel and figured those in charge of the event were relying on the good side of people's natures.

I bypassed the steadily growing line of people waiting to pay, then after submitting my ticket, held my hand out to be stamped with a red volleyball.

People were milling about in front of several long

tables placed end-to-end, covered with yellow tablecloths, and filled with a huge assortment of nicely organized items. A poster board listing details for the raffle was mounted to a large tripod sitting on the ground to the right. Melanie stood on the opposite side of the end table, taking money and handing out blue tickets.

"Hey, Melanie," I said, stepping up to the table after the woman in front of me moved aside. "It looks like you're staying busy." She was wearing the same outfit I'd seen earlier but had added a cap with a brim and a pair of sunglasses.

"Always." She puffed out a breath. "When it comes to charity events, the local businesses are always good about donating wonderful items, so we get a lot of traffic."

"Do you help with the raffles every year?"

Melanie grinned. "Ever since the committee came up with the idea."

I'd learned from Zoey that the annual tournament had been going on for the last seven years. I had to give Melanie points for her dedication. Though I'd never worked on a fund-raising committee, I knew it was hard work and took up a great deal of personal time.

I sensed people moving up behind me and didn't want to hold up the line. "I'll take ten tickets, please." I unzipped the pack on my hip and pulled some money out of my wallet.

"Once you find something you like, drop however many tickets you want into the container next to the item," Melanie said, handing back change and my half of the duplicate tickets. "Oh, and make sure to write your name on the tickets because this set,"—she wiggled the ones in her hand—"will go in the pot for a surprise drawing at the end of the event. You can use one of those pens if you don't have one." She pointed to a cup filled with an assortment of pens sitting near the end of her table.

"Thanks," I said, then started writing. "When's the drawing?"

"We usually wait until after the second game to allow latecomers to participate. You must be present to win." She used a stern tone to emphasize the last part. She'd most likely had people who hadn't paid attention in the past and complained when they missed out on winning something.

"Great," I said, then began perusing the wide selection, which included baskets, small fishing items, and souvenirs from some of the local gift shops.

I found a huge basket containing a variety of candies, most of them my favorites, donated by Dreamy Delectables. I'd just finished stuffing four of my last six tickets in a container when I heard Delia calling my name.

"I had a feeling you'd bid on that basket when I saw it earlier," she said.

"There's a lot of nice stuff here," I said, giving her a quick hug. "At this rate, I might have to buy more tickets."

Delia chuckled. "I'm not even going to tell you how much I spent on one of the baskets from Pemshaw's Pet Boutique."

Because of Harley, I frequented Leona's place regularly. Besides being a good friend of my aunt's, the woman's store was one of the places I enjoyed shopping. "Oooh, where are they?" I asked, glancing at the remaining tables I hadn't had a chance to peruse yet.

She tipped her head. "Come on, I'll show you. Or do you need to get more tickets first?"

The two tickets I held in my hand wouldn't be enough. "I'll be right back."

Delia chuckled. "I'll wait for you here."

Leona had donated two baskets, one with cat supplies and the other for dogs. After dispensing my additional tickets in the container for the puppy basket, I went with Delia to find Myrna, Vincent, and Harley.

We walked past the area where the games would be played. Team members for the Seagulls wore a variation of yellow shorts and tops. The Flounders dressed in similar attire but in green. A few people were doing stretching exercises, and others were practicing volleys over the net. Zoey had already arrived and stopped mid-stretch to wave.

The way the place had been arranged reminded me of a small carnival. There weren't any rides set up for children, but there were several concession trailers selling food and a couple of hand-built booths selling souvenirs, all lined up a reasonable distance from the playing area.

I wondered if the portable benches set up for spectators on one side of the net had been supplied by the town or on loan from a local high school. The opposite side of the playing field was beginning to fill with people who'd brought their own lawn chairs.

Our group had opted for seats near the ground on the bleachers. Sitting higher would've given us a better view, but being lower was more convenient. I wouldn't have to use the side stairs or hop over benches to get to the top if I needed to use the portable restrooms or take my dog for potty breaks.

Myrna, Vincent, and Delia were the best of friends. My aunt was in her fifties. She'd retired early and bought a beach-side home not long after receiving a sizeable settlement when she divorced my Uncle Craig.

Myrna and Vincent were long-time residents and also retired. Since it wasn't polite to ask someone's age, especially when they were older, I guessed them to be somewhere in their sixties.

I was the youngest member of our group, and even with the age difference, I enjoyed spending time with all of them. Since I was new to the area, I was still in the meeting people stage. Other than Zoey, who was a couple of years younger than me, I hadn't had time to form any other close friendships.

Myrna's outfit choices always made me smile. She usually wore purple socks with her favorite bright yellow tennis shoes. Today, however, the ones she wore were hot pink and didn't match her blue outfit.

Vincent stood above all of us by several inches and had thin wisps of hair covering his balding scalp. The majority of clothes in his wardrobe, at least the ones I'd seen, consisted of khaki shorts and Hawaiian shirts like the floral button-down top he was currently wearing.

They both were sitting on portable seat cushions, something I wish I'd thought to purchase before the game. I was accustomed to spending a good portion of my day on my feet. I was afraid my backside would rebel after being pressed against a hard metal surface for hours.

"Hi, guys," I said, giving them a small wave.

Harley had been napping on a folded, fluffy blue bath towel Myrna had placed on the ground for him. As soon as he heard my voice, he jumped up, his tail wagging so fast it wiggled the rest of his small body. His fur was mostly reddish-brown. There were patches of white around his muzzle, which also covered his chest and extended down the front of his legs.

"Hey there, boy," I said, crouching to scratch his head and receive doggy kisses. "Have you been behaving yourself for Myrna?"

"He's been great," Myrna said. "We already went for a walk so he could,"—she cupped the side of her mouth and lowered her voice—"do his business."

I wasn't sure if she thought talking about Harley's need to urinate would embarrass my dog or me, but her thoughtfulness was adorable and appreciated. "Thanks." I took the empty spot on her left, leaving space for Delia to sit next to me.

"It was sure nice of Archer to let you off early so you could see the volleyball game," Myrna said. "Is he planning on coming by later?"

"I doubt it," I said. According to my boss, if given a choice between watching people run around in the sand to hit a ball over a net versus a day spent tossing a hook and line in the ocean, deep-sea fishing would win every time. Unfortunately, by staying behind at the Bean, the closest he'd get to seeing any aquatic life today was in the shop's aquarium.

When I leaned forward to give Harley another head scratch so he'd settle back down on his makeshift bed, a shadow passed along the ground. Even with dark glasses, the sun's rays were bright, so I tilted my head back and held a hand over my eyes to speak to the older woman who'd stopped in front of us. "Good afternoon, Ellie."

She was also a retiree and lived a few blocks away from Delia. The strands in her bob-style haircut were an equal amount of brown and silver and curled inward, hitting the middle of her neck. The sun visor shading her dark eyes matched her pastel yellow short outfit. In her arms, she cradled Bruno, her white and tan Chihuahua. She had a large stuffed bag draped over her shoulder, and the bright blue leash clipped to Bruno's collar dangled from her wrist.

I didn't know if the dog got much exercise because Ellie carried him almost every time I saw them together. Not that I blamed her. There were a lot of pet owners in the area whose dogs were larger breeds and might view Bruno as an appealing snack.

I wasn't surprised to see her at the game. When I'd first visited Hawkins Harbor, before I knew I'd be moving here, she'd told me it was too bad I hadn't scheduled my vacation during the annual event.

"Is this seat taken?" Ellie asked. She didn't wait for a response before taking the spot on the other side of Vincent, causing him to furrow his brows and mumble an exasperated, "No." He wasn't a social person. Having someone as chatty as Ellie sitting next to him would make the rest of the day interesting.

Ellie leaned forward to see me around Vincent. "Brinley, why didn't you tell me your boyfriend would be playing today?"

Confused, I asked, "What boyfriend?" I was sure I'd be the first to know if I was in a serious relationship.

"Jackson, of course." She shifted in her seat and pointed at the team members gathered on the opposite side of the volleyball net. It was hard to miss the tall man with sandy blond hair huddled with some of the other members of the Frappuccino Flounders. Or the well-sculpted muscles not covered by his loose-fitting tank top and shorts.

My heart raced, and my stomach fluttered. "We're not," I stammered. "He's not…" The town's handsome vet and I had only been out to dinner a couple of times. I thoroughly enjoyed the time we'd spent together and wouldn't mind if our dating continued. Jackson was a super-hot guy who could have any woman he wanted. Heck, rumor had it that quite a few of the older women in the community had acquired pets so they could make appointments to get his attention.

After spending time with Jackson, I could understand why some of the town's females had resorted to sneaky measures. He was charming and had an appealing sense of humor.

Harley might have been responsible for my chance meeting with Jackson at the pet boutique, but I hadn't adopted him to wrangle a date with the vet. Still, I didn't want anyone to assume things had progressed to the point where we were considered an item. Not until I knew for certain that Jackson's interest wasn't fleeting.

I was about to argue further, but Ellie wrinkled her nose and said, "Uh-huh," in a disbelieving tone. Delia and Myrna giggled. Even Vincent, who rarely smiled, appeared amused.

I chanced another look in Jackson's direction, and as soon as his blue eyes met mine, he smiled. Embarrassed that I'd been caught staring, I ignored the warmth burning a trail across my cheeks and gave him a half-hearted wave. He said something to the guy standing next to him, then jogged around the net and padded barefoot through the sand in my direction. "Hi, everyone," he said, though his gaze stayed firmly on me.

During Harley's first visit to the clinic, he and Jackson had bonded in a friendly way. "Hey, Harley. Are you being a good boy?" Jackson asked as he bent down to lavish him with attention.

Harley whimpered happily, wagging his tail and shaking his entire body.

"I didn't know you played volleyball," I said after Jackson straightened. He hadn't mentioned anything about it the last time we went out.

Zoey liked to share things that happened in her life. She knew I'd gone out with Jackson, so I wondered why she hadn't said anything about him being on one of the teams.

"Normally, I don't," Jackson said. "I'm filling in for Tate Levine because he hurt his foot and can't play."

Injuries related to the feet, even if they were only sprains, could be painful. Having problems walking would only make it worse. "I hope he didn't hurt himself too badly."

"He's using crutches to get around. Between you and me, I don't think he really needs them. Tate seems to be getting extra attention from the ladies, so..." Jackson grinned and glanced to the other side of the playing area, where a guy was sitting on a lawn chair. One of his legs was stretched out, a medical boot covering the foot and ankle. Several young women were hovering nearby, laughing at something he'd said.

"I see," I said, unwilling to judge a guy I didn't know for using ingenuity. Though I wasn't sure why he'd need additional help. From what I could see, Tate had decent features and looked as if he spent quite a bit of time working out. "Are you two good friends?" Jackson and I were still in the getting-to-know-each-other stage, so I didn't know much about his personal life or the people he spent time with.

"No, only in passing," Jackson said. "I know Melanie,

the person in charge of the event. She's the one who asked me to fill in for Tate."

When I continued to watch, Jackson shifted to block my view. I couldn't tell by his fading smile if he harbored some jealousy or simply wanted my full attention. "My grandfather's here too," he said. "Would you like to meet him?"

My nervous flutters turned into a chest-tightening experience. I forced myself to keep breathing and tried to make the "Sure," I muttered sound convincing. Meeting the family of someone you'd just started dating always seemed awkward and added additional pressure. Jackson thought the world of his grandfather, and it would make things difficult if the man decided he didn't like me.

"Come on, I'll introduce you." Apparently, refusing Jackson's request wasn't an option. When he offered his hand to help me off my seat, I took it.

"Tell Griffin hello for me," Myrna said, grinning.

Jackson's grandfather had been her vet long before he'd moved to town to take over the practice. Griffin was supposed to be retired, but Jackson had told me he still took a few appointments for some of his older customers.

"I will," Jackson said as he held my hand and led me to the other end of the bleachers.

"Granddad," Jackson said. "This is Brinley."

Griffin's eyes sparkled with interest as he got to his feet. "Delia's niece, right?"

He stood a few inches taller than Jackson, which I estimated to be around six feet. Besides the silver hair and dark eyes, he possessed the same strong jaw and defined cheekbones as his grandson. I wondered if Jackson's father had equally striking features.

"It's nice to meet you, Mr. Walsh," I said.

"Please, call me Griffin." He held out his hand, his shake firm, his smile charming. I could see why my aunt and Myrna spoke highly of him.

We spent a few minutes chatting about my move and

my job with Archer before one of the male members of Jackson's team interrupted us. "Walsh, you playing or what?"

"Be right there," Jackson answered, then turned to me. "Come on, I'll walk you back."

I waited until we were almost to my seat before asking, "Are you afraid to leave me alone with your grandfather?"

Jackson didn't hesitate to respond with an emphatic yes.

"Oh," I said, trying to keep the disappointment out of my voice. I thought our short introduction had gone well. Had I somehow misinterpreted things?

"It's not what you think." Jackson stopped to take both my hands in his. "I don't want him to run you off by sharing all my embarrassing moments."

I chuckled. "I'm sure they can't be any worse than some of mine." Someone else on the team hollered Jackson's name, making him cringe.

"You better go before they come and drag you back," I said.

"Only if we can pick this up again later," Jackson said.

"Fair enough." I squeezed his hand. "Now go."

"Okay," he said, grinning as he backpedaled a few steps before sprinting off.

"How's Griffin doing?" Myrna asked once I settled back in my seat.

"Seems to be fine," I said.

"He's as good-looking as his grandson, don't you think?" She pretended to fan herself.

"It sounds like you have a little crush on the guy," I said.

Delia rolled her eyes. "More than a little."

Myrna shot a sidelong glare at my aunt. "Some people don't know what they're talking about."

"Uh-huh," Delia said, then tipped her chin toward the playing area. "Ooh, it looks like the players are getting ready to do their warm-ups."

"Vincent," Myrna said, reaching across my lap to pat his leg. "Do you have your miniature binoculars with you?"

"Yes, why?" He frowned. "Aren't your glasses working?"

"I can see just fine, thank you." She scowled. "I want to be ready when the shirts come off so I can get a closer look at all those muscles."

Delia rolled her eyes and shook her head. "You do realize some of the muscles you want to peruse belong to members of law enforcement, right?"

"If you're talking about Carson, then yes, I know." Myrna snickered. "I'd gladly let him arrest me as long as he did it without putting his shirt back on."

Carson was a deputy on the local police force, single, and quite handsome. When my aunt and her friends discovered I didn't have a boyfriend, they'd put him on their list of possible suitors. "Myrna, I'm appalled." I tried to sound serious even though I secretly looked forward to seeing the men flex their muscles. Especially Jackson.

"What?" She shrugged indignantly. "Being old doesn't equate to being a walking corpse. Some of my parts might be worn and sag a little, but they still work." Myrna wiggled her brows, leaving no doubt about which 'parts' she was referring to.

Delia groaned and swiped her hands down her shorts as she got to her feet. "This conversation has raised the temperature at least ten degrees. I'm going to pop over to Sharpe's and get something cold to drink." She pointed at the portable trailer belonging to Sharpe's Sandwiches and Snacks.

"I'll go with you," I said, turning to Myrna and Vincent. "Do either of you want anything?"

"Oooh, yes," Myrna said, widening her eyes. "I don't think they have red licorice, so I'd like two chocolate chip cookies and a large lemonade."

Her choice of sweet combined with sour didn't sound

appealing, but if it made her happy, I had no problem getting her what she wanted.

Myrna unzipped the pack near her hip and pulled out a five-dollar bill.

"I've got it," I said, waving away her offer to pay.

"Vincent...anything?"

"I usually have raspberry iced tea, but Zoey suggested I try the vanilla crème, so I'll have one of those," Vincent said.

I'd never sampled that flavor either, and I thought I might try it as well since the recommendation came from someone I trusted.

CHAPTER THREE

The Flounders had started their warm-up practice not long after Delia and I got in the line forming in front of the Shape's Sandwiches and Snacks trailer. From where we were standing, I still had a good view of the activities...and Jackson. The members of his team had taken positions on both sides of the net to do some volleying. He'd removed his shirt. His muscles rippled as he moved to intercept the ball.

Now that we were closer to the front of the line, I got a better view of the trailer. The window and counter sat higher off the ground than the constructed vendor booths. Besides the shop's name, the white metal exterior had an artfully painted mural of sandwiches and different kinds of cookies.

A trailer as nice as this was quite an investment for a business. I wondered if the owners participated in numerous events to offset the cost.

The couple in front of us stepped up to order, the man tall enough to rest one of his elbows on the counter. He was wearing a yellow tank top, and because he was standing sideways, I glimpsed part of the logo for the Seagulls on the front. The skin above his right cheekbone showed the fading purplish-yellow remnants of a bruise, which he could've sustained from a hit to the face during a practice game or maybe even a bar fight. Both reasons were suppositions since I'd never seen the man before and knew nothing about him.

The woman was several inches shorter than the man. Her shoulder-length blonde hair came from a bottle, the dark quarter-inch growth near her scalp revealing her natural color.

The woman inside the trailer appeared to be in her mid-thirties, with light brown hair fastened with a tie at her nape. She focused on swiping a cloth across a spill on the counter while asking, "Can I help you?"

"I hope so," the man said, grinning when the woman looked up and froze.

She double-blinked as if her imagination was playing tricks on her, then quickly recovered and narrowed her dark eyes at the man. "Derek," she said through gritted teeth. "What are you doing here?"

"I thought that was obvious, *Ivy*," Derek said sarcastically. "I want to place an order."

The woman beside him chuckled, the sound grating and filled with malice. Even though Ivy hid her flinch well and kept her eyes leveled at Derek, it was hard to tell if she knew the woman with him. "No, I mean, what are you doing in Hawkins Harbor?"

By the way they continued to glare at each other, I assumed they'd shared a history that hadn't been entirely good.

"I recently moved here, and I'm planning to start a new business," he said.

Ivy's face flushed, her anger evident. She crossed her arms. "What kind of business, and with whose money?"

I didn't usually practice the art of eavesdropping, but her comment piqued my interest. I hoped they'd share more details before realizing Delia and I were listening to their conversation.

"I don't think that's any of your concern," he said, scowling, his voice laced with disdain.

Ivy looked as if she wanted to argue. Instead, she inhaled a deep breath, then said, "If you were anyone else, I'd wish you luck with your endeavor. But we both know what happens to anyone who gets too close to you."

"Come on, Ivy," he said. "Don't be like that. You know we—"

She cut him off with a snarl. "I don't want to hear it, so please go."

The woman standing next to Derek whined, "But what about our order?"

Ivy closed her eyes as if trying to gain her composure. After a few seconds, she gave the woman a stern look and, in a strained but polite voice, said, "I'm exercising my right to refuse service."

Derek straightened and gripped the end of the counter. "We're not leaving until you fix us a drink."

Delia tensed, and I eased my hand to the zipper on my hip pouch. I was prepared to call for help if things turned ugly, or I should say uglier, since Derek was already causing a scene.

"You heard her, Derek," a male's voice, deep, threatening, and familiar, came from behind us.

I turned to see Brady Noonan striding towards us, determination in his steps. He was the owner of Noonan's Lawn Maintenance and also took care of Delia's yard. He possessed a similar height and body frame when compared to Derek's. I had no doubt if things escalated, the men would be equally matched.

When I'd first met Brady, my aunt told me he and his sister Avery, who worked as an events coordinator at the Promenade, had moved here from somewhere else. I wondered if that was how he knew Derek.

Brady glanced at Derek's shirt. "Shouldn't you be practicing? Or did you already get kicked off the team?"

Derek clenched his fists, the muscle in his jaw

twitching. "Still trying to be Ivy's knight in shining armor, I see."

"Just leave her alone," Brady said. It was obvious he wanted to say more, but he pursed his lips and tucked his hands into the pockets of his shorts instead.

Tension filled the air as the men glowered at each other. I was sure they'd end up in a fight, but Derek broke the silence first and said, "Fine. We'll go...for now."

"Word of advice, Natalie," Brady said, giving the woman with Derek a sympathetic look. "Derek's bad news, and if you're smart, you'll get away from him as quickly as possible."

Derek chuckled. "That's funny coming from you."

Natalie's face reddened. "You aren't going to let him talk to me like that, are you?"

"It's okay, sweetheart." Derek draped an arm across her shoulder. "He's not worth the effort."

Reluctantly, Natalie let him lead her away. "But she, they..." She shot a menacing glare over her shoulder at Ivy and Brady.

"Don't worry about it," Derek said. "I'll buy you something at one of the other booths."

Brady stared after Derek and Natalie until they disappeared into the nearest crowd. He gave Delia and me a brief nod, then said to Ivy, "I'll let you get back to it."

"Brady, wait," Ivy said, returning to the window a few minutes later with a tall to-go cup. She reached under the counter, pulled out a black marker, and then scribbled something on the side of the cup. "Here." She leaned across the counter and handed him the drink. "Thanks for...you know."

"Hero, huh," Brady said after reading what Ivy had written. If he'd taken a drink to disguise the crimson coloring his cheeks, it hadn't worked. "Anytime." When he strolled off, he headed in a different direction than the one Derek and Natalie had taken.

Had Derek been right about Brady's feelings for Ivy?

As far as I knew, Brady liked to flirt with women, myself included. I'd never seen him spend a lot of time with anyone, and I didn't think he had a steady girlfriend.

Delia stepped up to the order window. "Ivy, are you okay?" she asked in the same softened voice she used with me over the years whenever I seemed troubled. My aunt knew quite a few of the locals, so I wasn't surprised she knew Ivy.

"I'm fine," Ivy said. "I'm sorry you had to see that."

"Don't worry about it," I said. Without knowing the circumstances regarding their history, it was hard to tell if the shaking hand Ivy swept along the front of her apron was caused by anger or fear. Other than witnessing Derek's arrogance, I didn't have enough information to form an opinion about his personality. If he had a malicious side, he kept it well hidden.

Ivy's personal life wasn't any of my business. I knew I shouldn't get involved, but I needed to ease my concerns about the situation and maybe even her safety. I glanced around to make sure Delia and I were still the only people within earshot. "I don't want to seem nosy, but who was that guy?"

Ivy sighed. "My ex-husband, Derek. I moved here to get away from him and start over, but clearly that didn't work."

It was nice to know my instincts about their relationship had been accurate.

Ivy grabbed the cloth from underneath the counter again and wiped the already clean surface, an indication she wanted to avoid the subject.

Delia, being the understanding and perceptive person she was, also picked up on the change. "This is my niece, Brinley. She recently moved here too and is managing The Flavored Bean."

"It's nice to meet you. This is a great place to live," Ivy said, then mumbled, "At least it was."

I ignored the last part since I didn't think Ivy had

meant for us to hear it. "So far, I'd have to agree," I said.

"Now, what can I get for you?" Ivy said.

After Delia told Ivy what she wanted, I placed my order along with the items Myrna and Vincent had requested. The cookies she'd bagged for Myrna looked delicious, so I had her add two more for myself.

Just as we were leaving, the trailer's side door opened, and a man stepped inside. He stood a couple inches taller than Ivy and had a broader build. The similarities in the color of their hair and eyes, coupled with their facial features, made it easy to believe they were related.

"Hey, James," Ivy said. "Did Amelia send you to check up on me?"

He seemed oblivious to having an audience or that she'd asked him a question. "What was Brady doing here?"

Ivy turned to face him. "Please don't start." She rubbed her arms as she spoke.

Instead of heading back to our seats on the bleachers, which would've been polite and nonintrusive, Delia snagged my arm and pulled me to the side of the trailer and out of their line of sight. The move was something I expected from Myrna, not my aunt. I flashed her a curious look.

She held up a finger, so I followed her lead and strained to listen to James and Ivy's conversation.

"You know I don't want him hanging around you," James continued.

"Yeah, well, that's not up to you," Ivy said, her voice laced with irritation. "Besides, he's a paying customer."

"I don't care. He's no better than your ex." James paused. "And we know how that turned out."

"Thanks for reminding me," Ivy snapped.

"I..." James stammered. "Fine. I only stopped by to see if you needed a break."

"I'm good, but thanks."

"Okay, I guess I'll head back to the shop then," James said.

Ivy didn't seem to care that he'd softened his tone. "You do that," she snapped.

Delia waited until after the side door closed, then moved away from the trailer in a direction that would lead us back to the bleachers but keep Ivy from seeing us.

"I take it James and Ivy are related," I asked when we were halfway to our destination.

"Yes," Delia said. "They're brother and sister. James is older and a little overprotective."

"I noticed," I said. "Was that what prompted the covert eavesdropping?"

Delia ignored my admonishment. "After what Ivy told us about Derek, I wanted to make sure she wasn't going to have any problems with James."

From what I'd overheard of the sibling's conversation, James knew Brady and didn't think very highly of him or Derek. I wondered how he would've reacted if he'd walked in on the interaction between Ivy and her ex. Ivy might have considered the same thing, which would explain why she hadn't mentioned Derek's visit.

Delia's concern for Ivy had me worried. "Do you think Ivy's going to be all right?"

"I hope so," she said. "Maybe we should stop by the sandwich shop where she works in a day or so to check on her."

I hated to admit that I was getting as bad as Delia and Myrna when it came to mysteries, even those of a personal nature. Overhearing the exchange between Ivy, Derek, and Brady had left me with questions, and I knew I wouldn't be satisfied until I had the answers. "I think that's a great idea. Maybe we should see if Vincent and Myrna want to go with us."

CHAPTER FOUR

We'd been gone longer than I'd expected, and the game had already started by the time we got back. "What did we miss?" I asked as I handed Myrna and Vincent their stuff before taking my seat. Naturally, Harley smelled the cookies and was immediately on his feet, making a cute face and whimpering noises.

"Right now, the game is tied," Myrna said. "Too bad you missed the volley standoff between Carson and Jackson."

The men were on opposite teams and close in build. I was disappointed that I hadn't seen them facing off against each other.

"Who won?" Delia asked.

"Neither," Myrna said, taking a bite of her cookie.

"The ball ended up near Zoey, and she scored the point," Vincent said, then took a long draw from his drink. "Which currently puts them in the lead, but not by much."

Carson also played for the Seagulls. "How's the tea?" I asked since I hadn't tried mine yet."

"It's actually pretty good," he said. "Thanks for getting it for me."

I smiled because Vincent wasn't big on handing out

compliments. "Not a problem."

"Myrna, do you remember Ivy Sharpe?" Delia asked.

"Isn't she that nice gal who works at her brother's sandwich shop on the other side of town?" Myrna frowned. "Though, in my opinion, his wife's personality could use some work."

In other words, Myrna didn't think very highly of the woman, which I found interesting. I hadn't met James's wife and wondered what she'd done to earn my friend's unfavorable insight.

"Why did you want to know?" Myrna asked.

"Brinley and I found out that Ivy used to be married," Delia said. "Did you know?"

I was impressed my aunt had watched the game for another fifteen minutes after we'd returned before bringing up Ivy and her ex. Or maybe she'd been waiting for Ellie to leave on one of her many potty breaks for Bruno. Apparently, the little dog needed to go frequently. Either that or Ellie was making rounds to see her friends and gather gossip tidbits. My bet was on the latter since I saw her stop to chat with several people.

"Yes," Myrna said after she finished chewing another bite of her cookie. "I heard rumors that it ended badly, but I don't know the details. Why do you ask?"

"He's in town, and he showed up at Ivy's trailer while we were waiting in line," I said.

"I bet that went over well," Myrna said.

"Their interaction wasn't friendly." Delia pointed toward the game. "As a matter of fact, that's him covering the spot behind Zoey."

Myra leaned forward and squinted. "I don't recall ever seeing him before."

"That's because he's not from here," Delia said. "His name is Derek, and he recently relocated to Hawkins Harbor. He also told Ivy he planned to start a new business."

"Ivy didn't seem happy to hear the news," I said. "She

even refused to serve him." At least, I assumed the woman was his girlfriend based on how he treated her.

"Did things turn ugly?" Myrna asked.

"I think they might have if Brady hadn't shown up and asked Derek to leave," I said.

Myrna straightened her shoulders and grinned. "Do you think I should do some investigating?" Gossip was her specialty, and she occasionally tapped into the network of people living in the Promenade community.

"No," Delia said. "I don't think it's necessary." The unspoken word "yet" lingered in her tone. "Brinley and I planned to stop by her family's shop sometime this week to check on her. Would you like to come along?"

"Of course, I would," Myrna said. "Let me know when." She nudged Vincent in the arm. "You want to tag along too?"

"I'll have to check my busy schedule first," Vincent said. "But I think I can make it, provided there's a lunch involved."

Myrna snorted. They were both retired, so we all knew he had plenty of time available on his calendar. If the shop's sandwiches were as good as the cookies, then I wouldn't mind staying to eat.

A cheer ripped through the air from the people behind us, reminding me that I was missing the game again. We returned to watching the activities. Delia, Myrna, and I added cheers of our own. Harley was content to spend the remainder of the afternoon curled up in my lap, occasionally lifting his head when a ball landed in the sand close to us.

The afternoon passed quickly, and by the time Melanie announced the teams would be taking a short break, I was ready to stretch my legs and take Harley for a walk. I found an area not far from the beach that had been allocated for pet relief. After handing off the leash to Delia to seek the portable toilets and some relief of my own, I returned to the bleachers.

It seemed Brady wasn't the only one Derek had issues with. Not long after settling in the spot between Myrna and Delia, I noticed him having a heated discussion with a member of Jackson's team.

To pass the time until the game resumed, Vincent had pulled out his binoculars and was doing some bird-watching, specifically the seagulls, since they were the only winged creatures sailing through the overcast sky. I'd been preoccupied and hadn't noticed the dark clouds moving in our direction.

I leaned forward to get Vincent's attention. "I don't suppose you know how to read lips, do you?"

He lowered the glasses and wrinkled his nose. "Why?"

"I'd love to know what Derek and that guy over there are arguing about," I said, pointing.

Vincent adjusted the focus to zoom in closer. "It's not a skill I currently possess, but I wouldn't be opposed to learning."

He was voracious when it came to acquiring a new ability. I didn't doubt he'd become a master if he added the skill to his knowledge base.

"Judging by their body language, whatever they're discussing seems pretty serious," Vincent said.

Whatever they were arguing about abruptly came to an end when the sound of someone tapping a microphone echoed through the air, followed by Melanie's voice. "If I could have everyone's attention." There was a slight pause while she waited for people to stop talking. "Since the sunlight is dwindling and it looks like there's a storm brewing, the committee coordinators have decided to end the day's event." Her announcement was met with a lot of groans and boos.

"On the upside, the score is currently tied, so we'll have an additional game in the morning to determine this year's champions, and the game will be open to anyone who wants to attend." She waited for the crowd to stop cheering, then added, "We will go ahead with the raffle drawing now, so everyone, please head over to the tables."

It didn't take long for those anxious to see if they'd win to migrate to the area Melanie had specified. To keep things honest, she had selected a young woman to assist her. Starting at one end of the long tables, she systematically picked up the containers holding tickets and let the woman draw the winner.

Myrna squealed when her name was called, then disappeared through the crowd, returning a minute later with her arms wrapped around a cardboard box with a picture plastered on the side displaying a plastic toy castle.

"Don't you think Benjamin's a little old for toys?" Delia asked, referring to Myrna's nephew, who also happened to be the Promenade's manager and the only relative she ever talked about.

Myrna snorted. "It's for Ziggy." She held the box away from her chest to admire the picture. "I think he's going to love it."

"No doubt," I said, suppressing a giggle. I half listened as several more names I didn't recognize were called.

"Next, we have a set of dry-erase markers," Melanie said as she took a ticket from her assistant. "And the winner is Vincent Eldridge."

"I can't believe it," he said, then hurried toward the table to collect his prize.

Vincent rarely expressed happy emotions, but he displayed a hint of a smile as he strolled back to our group. "What?" he asked when he noticed our inquisitive looks. "At the rate we investigate, I didn't think having an extra set of markers handy would hurt." He lifted his chin, daring any of us to question his decision.

Our group got together once or twice a week to play the online game Crimes Galore Murder Mysteries. During the vacation leading to my relocation, I discovered that my aunt and her friends considered themselves sleuths and investigated some of the real crimes they learned about. Something that didn't make Carson happy and earned them, and me, numerous warnings.

Vincent had set up a whiteboard in Delia's home office during the first adventure they'd drawn me into. The board, which was still there and had seen some additional use, was primarily used to list suspects. I didn't want to ruin his enthusiasm and said, "Makes sense to me."

When Melanie moved to stand behind the baskets from Leona's place, I held my breath. I knew it was silly, but I truly wanted to win. Then I stood there staring in shock when Delia's name was called, shortly followed by mine.

I'd spent way more than I should've on tickets. It felt good to support an important cause, and I would've been okay even if I'd lost. Even so, winning was exhilarating, and I proudly snatched the puppy basket off the table.

Delia and I received envious glares when we carried our pet baskets back to the group. Since Myrna's hands were full, Vincent had taken my dog's leash when I'd gone to collect my prize. "What do you think, Harley?" I tipped the basket to show him the contents. Though he wagged his tail excitedly, I didn't know if he could smell the treats sealed beneath the clear cellophane.

"Hey," Jackson said when he joined us a few minutes later. He gave my basket an appreciative smile, then knelt down to scratch Harley's head. "It looks like you scored big, boy."

I waited for him to return to his feet, and, assuming he'd participated in the raffle, I asked, "How about you? Did you win anything?"

He grinned and retrieved a purple envelope from his back pocket. Printed on the outside in large, bold letters were the words **"Frigid Fantasy Flavors,"** along with several ice cream cone decals. He opened the envelope to show me the ten-dollar gift certificate stuffed inside.

"Congratulations," I said. We'd discovered during Harley's first visit to the animal clinic that he and I shared a fondness for the chilled treat.

"How many tickets did you have to buy to win that?" I

asked, still not feeling guilty about the small fortune I'd spent to get the puppy basket.

Cold sweets were popular when you lived in a hot and humid town. If he'd been like me, Jackson had most likely spent the equivalent or more to ensure he won.

"I'm not telling," he said, grinning mischievously and showing off his dimples. "But it was for a good cause, provided the woman I want to share this with agrees to go out with me."

I knew he was talking about me when he quirked an inquiring brow. My cheeks flushed. "I'm sure all a handsome guy like you has to do is ask." Once the color on his face matched mine, I added, "And supply a date and time."

CHAPTER FIVE

I started the day feeling refreshed from a good night's sleep and looking forward to watching the final game to see which team ended up winning the volleyball championship. Though my loyalties were torn because Zoey was on one team and Jackson on the other, I'd still be happy for whoever's team received the trophy.

I was also excited about my upcoming date with Jackson. We'd planned our ice cream outing for the following weekend when neither of us had to work, and we could take a leisurely stroll on the beach after we'd stuffed ourselves with chilly goodness.

Even having Luna attack my ankles from underneath the bed when I got up didn't put a damper on my day. Of course, I cringed when I heard the commotion she and Harley caused as they raced down the stairs. Delia was most likely already up and could run interference, but it didn't stop me from worrying about the breakable items she had in the living room.

Since I worked early most mornings, my aunt usually took Harley for his first walk. It was my day off, so I decided to spend some additional bonding time with my pet and get in a nice relaxing stroll at the same time.

The ground was damp from the rainstorm that had passed through the night. It hadn't rained hard enough to soak into the sand, but it did leave some small puddles on the sidewalks and streets. Now that the sun was out, it wouldn't take long for everything to dry off.

Our destination was usually the park located near the Promenade community, but I occasionally liked to change our route. I looked down at Harley, who happily paced next to me. We had plenty of time before the game was scheduled to start, so I asked, "How do you feel about doing something different this morning?"

I giggled, taking his cute doggy noises and tail wagging as an affirmative. "Okay then, exploring it is."

Instead of cutting through my aunt's neighborhood, I decided to go the long way around, which led past the beach area where the game would be played later. The plastic string of colorful pennant flags was still in place, and so were the vendor booths and trailers. The serving windows were all secured with panels, most likely to keep out any bad weather. If the owners were smart, they would've removed anything of value since I didn't think the panels would do much to deter possible thefts.

Melanie seemed like an efficient person, so I wasn't surprised to see that the raffle tables had already been taken down. I assumed she hadn't done the grand prize drawing to ensure more people returned for today's event. I was returning to watch the final game but was equally curious to see if I could win the final gift...whatever it was.

The beach and sidewalk were empty. The only sounds I heard were coming from the ocean's incoming waves and the squawks from seagulls flying overhead. Since there wasn't anyone around yet, I decided to let Harley get in a good run on the beach. I was about to unclip his leash when I noticed movement near the volleyball playing area.

The pole on the left side of the net was leaning sideways, and one of the corded ropes used to keep everything taut was being dragged across the sand by a playful orange-and-white-striped cat that looked awfully familiar.

"Quincy," I said, stepping off the sidewalk. "What are you doing way over here?" This section of the beach was quite a ways from the area near the Bean where he usually hung out. I wasn't an expert on stray cats, so maybe his territory was a lot larger than I'd thought. The aroma emanating from the different food places the day before was definitely an enticement for a curious kitty.

Harley barked and tugged on his leash. Quincy jerked his head in our direction. He released his new toy and bounded across the sand before disappearing behind one of the vendor booths. "Harley," I scolded. "You're supposed to be nice to Quincy, not scare him off."

My dog was notorious for chasing after the cat, but it had been more of a game. He'd gotten close to the animal several times but had never done anything to hurt Quincy, and I didn't think he ever would. He might have, however, set back my plans for befriending the feline.

Fixing the net before I left seemed like the right thing to do. I grabbed the dangling rope and was surprised when I didn't find a metal stake secured to the end.

Quincy didn't have the strength to pull the stake out of the ground or the fingers needed to free it from the rope. Maybe local teens had been responsible? Though I couldn't come up with a plausible reason why anyone would only steal a stake and not the entire net. Maybe it had come loose some other way and gotten covered with sand.

I scanned the nearby area for anything shiny but didn't find anything. I'd been so busy concentrating on my task that when a repetitive squeak echoed through the air, it startled me. I spun around, nearly tripping over Harley, and spotted Ivy wheeling a handcart stacked high with sealed plastic containers along the sidewalk.

"Hey, Ivy," I said, plodding through the sand to join

her.

"Good morning, Brinley," Ivy said as she balanced the stack and raised the cart into an upright position.

Harley rarely met anyone he didn't like. He whimpered and wagged his tail, anxious to draw Ivy's attention.

"Who's this?" She leaned over, offering her palm for him to sniff.

"Harley."

"He's adorable." Ivy scratched his head once he'd given her hand an approving lick.

"Thanks. I think so too." I glanced at the cart. "You're here early. Are you expecting another busy day?"

"I have no idea. This is the first game I've helped with." She leaned on the cart and sighed. "Even if I end up standing around the whole time, it'll be worth it since I won't have to listen to Amelia's ranting."

"Who's Amelia?" I asked.

She giggled. "I'm sorry, I forgot you haven't lived here that long and haven't experienced an unfortunate introduction yet. She's my sister-in-law...and a total harpy." Her smile faded, and she shook her head. "I don't know what my brother ever saw in her."

"I take it she doesn't make your life easy," I said.

Ivy snorted. "Not one little bit. You should have heard her yesterday when I told her I'd run into Derek and he'd moved to town. I wasn't happy about the news, but I thought she was going to have a meltdown."

"I take it she doesn't like him much," I said.

"That would be an understatement. I'd say borderline hate would be a better way to describe it." Ivy bit her lower lip and looked as if she might provide more information, then quickly changed the subject. "So, what brought you out here this early?"

"I usually take Harley for a walk in the park, but we decided to do a little exploring," I said, smiling down at my dog. "I noticed the sagging net and was trying to fix it when you arrived."

Ivy glanced past my shoulder and frowned. "That's not good. Melanie is going to be furious when she sees it. Do you want some help?"

"I don't think there's anything we can do. It looks like one of the stakes is missing," I said. "I hope she keeps a spare set of parts handy; otherwise, the game will be delayed."

"I wouldn't worry." Ivy chuckled. "She's pretty organized."

"How about you?" I asked, wiggling a finger at her cart. "Do you need some help?"

"No, but thanks," she said, pressing a hand on the top container as she tipped the cart back. "Are you coming to the game later?"

"I wouldn't miss it." I stepped back so she could roll the cart through the gap between the string of flags. The wheels weren't cooperating in the sand, so Ivy turned around and maneuvered it backward. After flashing me a smile, she disappeared behind her trailer.

A few seconds later, I heard a heart-wrenching scream. Ivy reappeared without her cart. Her face had turned a sickly shade of white. She stumbled toward me, gasping for air and clutching the front of her T-shirt.

The first thing to pop into my mind was an article I'd read not long ago about some people who'd spotted an alligator sunning itself on a beach. None of the locals had ever mentioned seeing one before, but there was always a first time. "Ivy, what's wrong?" I asked, hurrying to meet her halfway.

Ivy gripped my arm hard enough to leave impressions from her nails. "He's, he's...dead." She pointed at her trailer.

I shuddered. "Who's dead?" I hoped she was mistaken and had inadvertently encountered someone who'd fallen asleep on the beach.

Ivy swallowed hard, then took a deep breath before rasping, "Derek." Whatever history they'd shared, it was obvious she hadn't completely despised him. If she didn't care about him, even subconsciously, I'd have expected her reaction to be different—colder.

I needed to see what she'd found for myself, but Ivy clearly wasn't in any condition to go with me. I was more concerned with her mental state and hoped that giving her something else to focus on would prevent her from going into shock. I slipped the end of my dog's leash off my wrist and handed it to her. "Would you mind staying here and looking after Harley?"

"Okay." She nodded, appearing relieved.

If Derek was truly dead, his wouldn't be the first body I'd seen this year. He'd be the second. Even so, it didn't make slipping behind the trailer and taking a look any easier.

The cart was sitting upright, but the containers had toppled off. Beyond the heap of plastic, a man was lying on the ground, facing away from me. My nerves were on edge, and the calming breath I took didn't help the anxiety thrumming through my system.

"Derek," I said. When I didn't get a response, I slowly crept forward until I could get a look at his face. Seeing his dark eyes locked in a death stare was unnerving. It wasn't nearly as unsettling as seeing his hand wrapped around the missing stake protruding from his chest right through the Seagull logo on his yellow tank top. Or the dark, bloody spot that had seeped into the sand near his body.

Derek's hair and clothes looked damp. A thin layer of moisture covered the exposed skin still shaded by the trailer. Did that mean he'd been killed before it had rained? Had Derek known his killer, or was the attack a surprise?

The only way to know for sure would be to move his body and check the sand underneath. I didn't want to be lectured about tampering with a crime scene, so I didn't touch anything.

I'd seen how he treated Ivy and got the impression it was a milder version of their interactions. The fact that she'd moved to another town to get away from him supported my theory. What if Derek had a history of crossing others in a similar fashion? Would it give someone enough of a motive to want him dead? What didn't make sense was the location or the way he'd been killed. Was the killer hoping he'd be found by Ivy or another member of her family?

Whatever the circumstances, the scene was gruesome, and I had to gulp more air to keep the bile from rising in my throat. I also needed to report the death to the authorities and call Delia to let her know what happened.

Once I told my aunt and our friends about Derek's death, they would bombard me with questions pertaining to what I'd seen.

The look I'd gotten of the body was already imprinted in my mind and would most likely stay there for a very long time. Sticking around and searching for clues wasn't an option. I gave the surrounding area a quick perusal, taking in as many details as possible.

That's when I noticed a to-go cup with the Sharpe's sandwich shop logo lying on its side not far from the trailer. The town was pretty adamant about keeping the beaches clean. I hadn't seen debris anywhere else, so I didn't think it was leftover trash from the game.

I squinted to get a better look and gasped when I saw the words "My hero" handwritten in black at an angle. It had to be the same cup Ivy had given Brady the day before. I didn't want to believe Brady was responsible for Derek's death. Surely, he'd thrown it away once he'd finished his drink rather than keeping it as a memento. Even if he had kept the cup, how did it end up here?

Had Ivy seen the cup when she spotted the body? Would she have removed it if she had?

Fighting the urge to pick up the cup and examine it, I slowly retraced my steps. As soon as I cleared the end of the trailer, I checked to make sure Ivy was all right. She was standing where I'd left her, had picked up Harley, and was cuddling him as if he were her favorite stuffed animal. My dog was great at snuggling and seemed to help with keeping Ivy calm.

After flashing her a supportive look, I retrieved the cell from the pouch on my hip. I tapped the speed dial button for Carson's mobile, a number I'd acquired from being involved in a couple of his cases.

He answered after two rings. "Brinley, please tell me this is a social call."

The only time Carson and I talked socially was in public and usually when he stopped by the Bean to get a to-go coffee before work. "I wish I could," I said.

When he groaned, I imagined him scowling and pinching the bridge of his nose. "Let's have it," he said. There was rustling in the background, and I assumed he must be getting dressed.

This wasn't the first dead person I'd had to report. I didn't want him to think I purposely scoured the beaches looking for bodies, so I decided providing some backstory might be helpful. If nothing else, it would make me feel better not to be treated like a suspect. I started by telling him about my early morning walk with Harley, then progressed to the condition of the volleyball net and running into Ivy.

"So, you're saying Ivy's the one who found the body? And it's Derek, her ex-husband?" he asked. His voice was brusque and suggested that my additional commentary hadn't been necessary.

"Yes," I said. "I checked to make sure, but I didn't touch anything." I didn't give him any explicit details about the stake or the blood in the sand since he'd be able to see for himself when he arrived.

"You know the routine. I'll be there shortly," he said, then disconnected the call.

As disheartening as it was, I did know what to do. I slipped my phone back into my pouch and walked over to wait with Ivy. Finding a body was traumatic. I could only imagine how it must feel if it was someone a person had once been close to. Derek and Ivy might not be together anymore, but there had to be a time when they'd cared enough about each other to take marital vows. I placed my hand on Ivy's arm. "Are you doing okay?" Her face had regained some color, but I still worried about her going into shock.

"I think so," Ivy said. "Is he... Is Derek dead?" She sounded hopeful, as if what she'd seen hadn't been true.

"I'm afraid so." I scratched Harley's head. "I called the police. Carson wants us to wait right here."

I was about to congratulate myself on being lucky that no one else had walked by yet when I heard Melanie calling mine and Ivy's names.

"You're here early." Melanie's tone held a hint of chastisement as if the beach wasn't open to the public and we had no right to be there.

"What's wrong?" she asked as soon as she noticed the smeared mascara Ivy's crying had caused on her face. "What happened?"

Ivy shook her head. A new tear trickled down her cheek. When she opened her mouth to speak, all she managed was a squeak.

"I'm afraid there's been a death," I said.

"Who?" Melanie asked.

"My ex, Derek," Ivy mumbled.

Melanie shot her a skeptical look, then gave the area a quick glance. "Where? I don't see a body."

"That's because he's behind my brother's trailer," Ivy said.

"Show me," Melanie said.

"We can't." I stepped in front of Melanie to keep her from checking out the scene herself. "The police are on their way, and Carson instructed me to keep everyone back until he gets here."

Melanie crossed her arms and stuck out her chin defiantly. "But I'm in charge of the event. I have a right to know what's going on."

"Your 'event' is now a crime scene, and I guarantee you the police won't be happy if you tamper with anything. Which includes leaving more footprints in the sand." It was bad enough that mine and Ivy's prints were already near the body.

Melanie slapped her hands on her hips and challenged me with a narrow-eyed glare. I held my position a few more seconds, then stepped out of the way. Carson hadn't said anything about wrestling people to the ground if they chose not to listen. I wasn't a scrapper by nature, and she was carrying a few extra pounds that might push things in her favor if things progressed to a tussle. If Melanie wanted to risk tangling with local law enforcement, I wasn't about to stop her.

Instead of pushing past me, Melanie relented and said, "I suppose you're right, but I'm not leaving."

I was already emotionally exhausted. Once Carson arrived, things would only get worse. Having a little support wouldn't hurt, so I retrieved my phone again, this time calling my aunt.

As soon as Delia answered, I said, "You won't believe what's happened."

CHAPTER SIX

It was almost a tie between who arrived at the crime scene first. Carson beat Delia, Myrna, and Vincent by a couple of minutes. I stayed close to Ivy and kept an eye on Melanie, prepared to remind her about police procedures again if she changed her mind about seeking out Derek's body.

Harley was happily sniffing the sand near my feet. He liked affection but would only tolerate being held for a short period of time. He'd grown tired of being clutched against Ivy's chest and squirmed until she put him down.

Douglas Dankworth, the newest member of the police force, showed up fifteen minutes after everyone else. The first time we'd met was right after I'd found a body buried on the beach. This time he'd come prepared with stakes and yellow police tape. No doubt a result of the scolding he'd received the last time when he'd forgotten to bring the necessary items to cordon off the crime scene.

A jogger and several people out walking had taken note of the activities but were politely asked to move to the opposite side of the street and out of the way. I'd seen at least one person pull out their cell phone and knew it wouldn't be long before news of Derek's death made its way through town.

After Carson checked to make sure Ivy was all right and told her not to leave because he'd need a statement once he secured the crime scene, he pulled me aside and out of earshot of the others. He narrowed his intense gaze at Myrna, Vincent, and Delia, then scowled at me. "When you called me, you didn't say anything about sending for backup."

I found his use of cop lingo, especially with a civilian like me, amusing, and I tried not to smile. "They're not backup; they're moral support. I needed to let Delia know I was running late so she wouldn't worry," I said. "Besides, finding a body is traumatizing, even if it's only my second one." Not that I wanted there to be any more dead people in my future.

Carson rolled his dark eyes. "So why are Vincent, Myrna, and Melanie here?" he asked.

"Myrna and Vincent are like family; they were concerned about me," I said. "Melanie showed up on her own right after our call ended."

Carson closed his eyes and rubbed his forehead, a sign my explanation wasn't convincing. When he opened his eyes again, I was certain he'd order my friends and me to leave. Instead, he gritted his teeth and snarled, "Fine. I may have more questions, so I'd like you to stay." He held up his hand. "But I'm holding you responsible for keeping them out of the way." He walked off, his stride filled with purpose and possibly some frustration.

"What's the verdict?" Delia asked as soon as I returned to the group.

"Carson wants me to stick around in case he has more questions," I said. It was okay with me because I preferred talking to him here rather than being interrogated at the station. Something Delia and I'd already experienced when Carson questioned her about her relationship with Myles Mumford, the dead guy Harley and I found on the beach shortly after moving here.

"I think we're growing on him," Myrna said.

I giggled. "Yeah, I'm sure that's it."

"Did Carson say anything about continuing the volleyball game?" Melanie asked.

Melanie's lack of empathy was troubling. "No," I said, giving her a disbelieving glance. I'd have thought it was obvious the event was temporarily canceled after watching Douglas string the police tape. Did the woman actually need to see the body to realize a crime had been committed?

It seemed Melanie wasn't satisfied with my answer. She rushed after Carson and caught him before he could slip back under the tape. After a brief discussion that didn't appear to go in her favor, Melanie stomped in our direction, her lips pursed so tight her mouth almost disappeared.

"I take it he canceled the volleyball game," I said.

"Yes," Melanie huffed. "He also had the nerve to tell me he'd have me escorted from the area if I went anywhere near his crime scene again."

I wanted to ask her what she expected. Instead, I said, "I'm sure he understands your dilemma. Carson's efficient and good at his job. He'll push things along so you can finish your event in a day or two."

My words of encouragement didn't seem to impact Melanie in the slightest. She continued to frown as if I'd mumbled gibberish.

"Brinley's right," Delia said, gently touching Melanie's arm. "This isn't your fault, and the other committee members will understand."

"I hope you're right," Melanie said, her tone less irritated than it was before.

Once again, I was impressed with my aunt's ability to deduce the root of Melanie's anger—her reputation. Derek's death was an inconvenience and had ruined the smooth execution of her event.

I knew my friends were anxious to hear what I'd seen,

but I didn't want to share any details in front of Melanie. Luckily, they didn't either, so we all waited quietly, staring at the trailer and waiting for Carson to return.

After spending time on the crime scene, Carson emerged from behind the trailer. He stopped to give Douglas instructions, then motioned for Ivy to follow him to a spot away from our group. She seemed reluctant to go, and I'd thought about offering to let her take Harley with her.

Hearing someone call for their mother had all of us looking toward the woman I'd seen with Derek the day before. She raced along the sidewalk and stopped in front of Melanie. "Is it true? Is Derek dead?"

"Yes," Melanie said, then her daughter into a hug.

This was quite the development. I had no idea the two women were related. Melanie was a couple of inches taller than Natalie. Now that they were standing next to each other, I could see similarities in their facial features; the same brown eyes and slant to their noses.

"It's just like the man to ruin things for everybody," Melanie said.

"Mom, that's not fair," Natalie said, swiping at the tears on her face. "Derek wasn't all that bad."

"Really?" Melanie narrowed her eyes about to argue, then must've realized the rest of us were standing there, listening. "We'll talk about it later." She turned to my aunt. "Delia, have you met my daughter, Natalie?"

Technically, observing Natalie and Derek's interaction with Ivy the day before wasn't an introduction. Clearly, my aunt wasn't any more unimpressed with the younger woman than I was. Delia offered a tight smile, then said, "No, but it's nice to meet you." She touched my shoulder. "This is my niece, Brinley." She swept her arm to the other members of our group. "And our friends Myrna and Vincent."

I'd expected Natalie to recognize us, but her attention was focused elsewhere, and she brushed off the introductions by muttering, "Uh-huh."

Natalie pointed toward the spot where Carson was still questioning Ivy. "What's she doing here?"

"Supposedly, Ivy's the one who found Derek's body," Melanie said sarcastically.

Natalie sniffled. "She's probably the one who killed him."

I'd already gleaned that something bad had happened between Ivy and Derek. Something he might have shared with his current girlfriend. "Why do you say that?" I asked, hoping she'd elaborate.

"I found out yesterday that she's Derek's ex," Natalie said, disdain lacing every word. "He told me they had a bad marriage, and their divorce was even worse. He also said that Ivy blamed him for having to leave Clarksburry and move here to live with her brother."

I wasn't familiar with that town and planned to look up its location later. I shared an inconspicuous look with Delia. There was more to the story than Derek had shared with Natalie. People didn't relocate without a good reason. I should know since my move to Hawkins Harbor resulted from Stacy Adler, the CEO's daughter at the last place I was employed, interfering with my work life. In my case, the outcome had been a good one. I wasn't so sure if Ivy could say the same.

I was curious to find out what had happened between Ivy and Derek. If after they'd split up, and Ivy had relocated to get away from him, then what made him decide to move here? Had he been secretly stalking Ivy? I didn't think that was likely since he'd already taken up with Natalie. Maybe it was the business venture Derek had mentioned.

I thought about asking Natalie for more details but didn't want to seem too nosy. Based on her low opinion of Ivy, the information might be biased and not entirely the truth.

News traveled fast, and it wasn't long before more

people started gathering. After witnessing how protective Brady had been of Ivy, I wasn't surprised when he showed up a few minutes later. I was, however, shocked to see him hurry in Carson's direction. Something had happened in Brady's past that got him into trouble with the law, and he usually avoided Carson. Maybe Brady's feelings for Ivy went deeper than a concerned friend.

Finding the body and her connection to the dead guy made Ivy a possible suspect. Given Brady's history and his argument with Derek, I was pretty sure he'd be undergoing some heavy scrutiny from Carson. Even more so if the police ran tests on the cup and found Brady's prints and DNA all over it.

Natalie didn't miss Brady's arrival either. She stabbed a finger in his direction and said, "Or maybe Ivy got him to take care of Derek for her." The vehemence in her voice made me cringe. The more time I spent around Natalie, the less I liked her and the drama she created. Before she caused a scene that would start unnecessary rumors, I said, "I don't think it's a good idea to make accusations without knowing all the facts."

"Facts," Natalie practically shrieked as she jerked her head to glare at me. "You were there. Don't you remember how he treated Derek and me yesterday?"

I wasn't sure how I felt about finally being recognized or used to further her theatrics. She'd conveniently forgotten Derek's role in creating the situation. He could've taken Natalie to one of the other vendors serving beverages, yet he'd chosen the one where his ex-wife worked.

Brady and Derek might have shared a few verbal barbs, but neither of them had gotten aggressive or escalated their confrontation into a physical fight. Not that it wouldn't have happened if there hadn't been a bunch of people hanging around. Delia and me included.

Even though I'd had limited contact with Natalie, I'd already discerned that reasoning with her would be impossible. I tried diplomacy, hoping to prevent hysterics. "It sounded like a misunderstanding to me." I shrugged and made an empathetic face. It obviously hadn't worked because she harrumphed and crossed her arms, a mannerism mirroring the one her mother had used earlier.

Melanie didn't seem to appreciate my efforts either. "We have to let the police do their job. "They'll figure out what happened," she said, draping her arm across her daughter's shoulder. "Carson will most likely question everyone who attended the game yesterday." She glared at me as she spoke. "You'll be able to tell him your side of the story."

I could only imagine what Natalie's fabricated version would sound like. I wanted to add that the police would be able to do it a lot faster if everyone they spoke with told them the truth. Once again, I found myself forcing a smile and holding my tongue.

Myrna, on the other hand, showed no restraint. She held her hand near her mouth and muttered, "Hopefully, no more lies will be spewed."

I faked a cough, hoping to cover up her comment. Carson had limited resources and couldn't track down all the people who'd watched the game so he could interrogate them. Natalie would most likely be questioned because of her relationship with Derek. Carson was intelligent and perceptive. He'd undoubtedly see through her antics and any twisted version she offered.

Members from both teams started to arrive. Jackson wasn't among them, but Zoey was. As soon as she spotted us, she quickened her pace to reach us. She had her hair pulled back into a ponytail and was wearing gym shorts and her team's tank top. "What's going on?"

"My boyfriend was murdered," Natalie shrieked.

"What?" Zoey asked, dropping the gym bag she was carrying near her feet. "Are you saying Derek's dead?"

I shook my head and was about to explain, but Melanie cut me off. "I need to speak with the players and let them know the game has been canceled." She gave her daughter a stern look. "Natalie, please go home. I'll check in on you later." She hurried off, not waiting to see if her daughter would comply.

It seemed that Natalie had a rebellious nature because she ignored her mother's request. I spent the next few minutes catching Zoey up with the details, talking fast to keep Natalie from interrupting me.

"That's terrible," Zoey said after I finished. "I'm so sorry, Natalie."

"Thanks," Natalie said, wiping away the fresh tears streaming down her face. She returned to watching Ivy, who now stood off to the side with Brady. Carson had finished questioning the couple and was overseeing the crime scene and the medical personnel who'd shown up with a gurney to remove the body.

The way she was glaring, I worried she might decide to cause a scene. "Natalie," I asked. "How long were you and Derek together?"

She blinked, then pulled her gaze away from Ivy. "A couple of months. We got together right after he moved here." Natalie went back to sniffling again. "He had big plans."

"Really?" I pretended I hadn't overheard him say something about opening a business to Ivy the day before. "Like what?"

Natalie slumped her shoulders and stared at the ground. "I guess it doesn't matter now."

I held back a groan. Was it possible Derek's new business venture had something to do with his death? There was no way of knowing without more details, and now wasn't the time to try coaxing them out of Natalie. Not with more people arriving, including the guy quickly approaching us who'd played on Jackson's team yesterday. He was also the person I'd seen arguing with Derek during the intermission between the games.

"Hey, Jacob," Zoey said.

"Hi," he said, bulldozing past both of us to reach Natalie. "I'm sorry about Derek. Are you all right?" Jacob's dark eyes flickered with concern. He pulled Natalie into a hug that lasted longer than necessary for someone comforting a friend.

"I...don't know." A new batch of tears trickled down Natalie's face. "I guess so." She placed a hand on his arm. "What about you? He was your friend. Are you handling things okay?"

"Yeah," Jacob mumbled.

Maybe I'd imagined Jacob's cringe when she'd mentioned the two males being close. Since Zoey had grown up in Hawkins Harbor and played volleyball with Derek and Jacob, she might have better insight into their relationship. She might even know what had caused their disagreement, but I'd have to wait until later to ask her.

Right now, it looked like Carson and Douglas were taking names and asking people to leave, which I'm sure would eventually include my friends and me.

CHAPTER SEVEN

Derek's death happened to fall on the same day our group usually got together at my aunt's place to play our online mystery game. After a light meal, we'd decided to skip playing and move on to discussing his murder.

Delia had transformed one of her extra bedrooms into an office that looked more like an entertainment area. Her computer, monitor, and keyboard were sitting on a desk in a corner near the window. The other half of the room had a television mounted to the wall, the screen facing a cushioned sofa wide enough to comfortably seat three people, and a matching chair positioned to the right. The wooden rectangular coffee table made serving snacks and drinks convenient.

The tripod and whiteboard Vincent had brought to our first gathering were still sitting near the wall, not far from the screen. As soon as we entered the room, he added the colored markers he'd won in the raffle to the ones already stored with the board.

While I plopped down in the chair, Vincent, Myrna, and Delia took their usual places on the couch. Since we didn't bring any food with us, Harley wouldn't be able to practice his begging skills, so he settled on the floor near my feet.

"Okay, let's have it," Myrna said.

"And don't leave out any details," Vincent added.

Their request wasn't unexpected, but I was glad they'd waited to ask until we were done eating. I would've lost my appetite if I'd had to describe the gruesome sight I'd found when I walked behind the Sharpe's trailer. Unpleasant as it was, I spent the next ten minutes telling them everything I could recall, starting with Ivy's arrival and ending with the to-go cup I'd spotted in the sand.

I could tell by their expressions that they were anxious to share their opinions but were politely holding back until I finished.

"Did either of you know Derek?" I directed my question at Vincent and Myrna since I already knew Delia's answer.

"No," Vincent said.

"Me neither," Myrna said.

"I didn't even know Ivy had been married until yesterday," Delia said.

"I know spouses, even an ex, are usually the ones who did it," Myrna said. "Ivy's such a sweet person. I can't imagine her being capable of killing anyone."

"I don't either," I said. "Derek and Ivy might have had a bad marriage, but her reaction to finding his body had seemed genuine." Unless a person truly despised someone, I wanted to believe they'd still care about what happened to them, even if only a little.

"Are you sure the cup you saw on the ground belonged to Brady?" Vincent asked. "He doesn't seem like the type of guy to save a to-go cup from a woman, no matter how much he liked her."

"Maybe so, but I don't think Ivy randomly scribbled the words "My hero" on all the cups she handed out," I said.

"What if the person who wanted Derek dead decided to frame Brady," Myrna said. "Maybe they followed him, then dug the cup out of the trash."

"Sounds a little morbid," Vincent said, scratching his chin. "But I suppose it's possible. It's too bad you didn't think to snap some pictures with your phone. A visual layout of the scene would've been helpful."

I rolled my eyes, not sure how to take his comment. He thought digging around in the trash was disgusting, but getting an image of a dead guy and the bloody sand beside him was okay. "I'll try to remember that the next time I find a body," I said sarcastically.

His eyes sparkled with amusement, and though he rarely smiled, the ends of his lips lifted slightly.

We'd already established that none of us knew Derek personally. If someone had actually gone through the trash, coming up with their identity might be impossible. "Derek and Natalie had already gone by the time Ivy wrote on the cup. Besides you and me, who else could've seen her give it to Brady?" I asked my aunt.

"I'm afraid I wasn't paying attention," Delia said. "I was too busy ordering."

Thanks to my aunt, we'd also been eavesdropping on the conversation between James and Ivy, which I wasn't about to mention because I didn't want to risk embarrassing her.

"Besides being her ex, did Ivy tell you anything useful about Derek?" Vincent asked.

"According to Natalie, he moved here a couple of months ago," I said. "Ivy didn't know anything about it and acted like it was the first time she'd seen him in town. She didn't sound happy when Derek mentioned starting a new business."

"That's right." Delia snapped her fingers. "She even asked him where he planned to get the money."

"Did he tell her?" Myrna asked.

"No," Delia said. "Things got a little tense after that."

The melodic sound from the doorbell echoing through the room startled me more than Harley barking and racing into the hallway. Delia sprang to her feet. "I'll get it."

"Were we expecting someone else?" Myrna asked.

"Not that I know of," I said, straining to listen to the voices coming from the front of the house.

A few minutes later, my aunt returned with Zoey. Whatever had been shared between them must've been upsetting because Delia flashed me a concerned look when she entered the room.

Zoey sometimes joined our group, but she usually called first. Her hair was down, and she'd changed into a short-sleeved shirt and jeans. "Err," she growled as she stomped into the room and dropped a small to-go box and bag from Tori's Tasty Treasures on the coffee table. I worried that the contents, which were hopefully slices of cheesecake, had survived the landing.

Food was always Harley's top priority. He sat on the floor and eyed the box. If he'd sensed Zoey's troubled demeanor, he ignored it.

She was normally an even-tempered person. Something monumental must've happened to affect her mood. "What's wrong?" I asked.

"Natalie. That's what," Zoey snapped.

"What did she do?" After witnessing Natalie's earlier dramatics, it could've been anything.

Zoey groaned. "She's going around town telling anyone who'll listen that Brady killed Derek."

"That's awful," Delia said.

"I think someone should shove a scone in her mouth," Zoey said. "Maybe that would keep her quiet."

Judging by her frown and clenched fists, I was certain Zoey would be the first to volunteer. I didn't want to make my friend any madder than she already was, but Natalie was connected to Derek. Getting some background information on her would be helpful. "Have you known Natalie long?" I asked.

"Yeah," Zoey sighed, releasing some of her frustration. "We went to high school together. She wasn't any better back then either." She waved away the office chair Delia had rolled out from behind the desk, then sat cross-legged on the floor next to the table. Zoey pulled Harley onto her lap. Once she was done nuzzling him, she asked, "You guys don't think Brady's responsible, do you?"

"We were discussing that very thing right before you arrived," Myrna said. "And no, we don't."

"Thanks for bringing us dessert, Zoey," Delia said, stepping into the role of hostess as she removed the plates, napkins, and utensils from the bag and placed them on the table.

"I was going to call, but then I overheard what Natalie had said about Brady, and I forgot," she said.

"You're always welcome anytime, so don't worry about it." Delia swept from the room, returning a few minutes later with a bottled water for everyone.

Tori's baked goods were awesome. Her cheesecake drizzled with chocolate was some of the best I'd ever tasted. Myrna was the closest to the box, so she leaned forward and started dishing out the contents.

Other than a few appreciative noises, the first few bites everyone took of their dessert were shared in silence.

Now that Zoey had calmed down, I figured it was safe to ask her some questions. I took a long swig of water, then asked, "How well did you know Derek?"

She lowered her fork. "Not very. I didn't meet him until he signed up to play volleyball. I might be wrong, but I think he only joined to impress Natalie's mom."

After hearing Melanie's earlier comments, I was certain his attempts hadn't been successful. "What can you tell us about the relationship between Jacob and Derek?"

Zoey wrinkled her nose. "Why do you ask?"

"I saw them arguing during intermission yesterday and was curious what it could've been about."

"I have no idea. Anytime I've seen them together, they seemed to get along all right," Zoey said.

"Do you think it had something to do with Natalie?" I

asked.

Zoey shrugged. "Maybe. I know Jacob and Natalie used to date. She says they're just friends, but I think he still might have a thing for her."

That would explain his overprotective manner at the crime scene. Any further questions I'd intended to ask slipped from my mind when the doorbell rang for the second time. Delia and I shared a confused look. "Were you expecting someone else?" I asked.

"Not that I'm aware of," Delia said, already on her feet and heading for the hallway. Harley bounded after her. Like before, I couldn't tell from the mumbled voices who'd arrived. "Look who's here," Delia said a few minutes later as she led Avery into the room. Since she didn't have any food, Harley trotted past her and returned to his spot near my feet.

Avery glanced around the room and nervously tucked some blonde strands behind her ear. "I know I should've called first."

Anytime I'd ever seen her, which was usually at one of the Promenade events, she'd been professionally dressed. Tonight, she was wearing a pair of shorts, a worn T-shirt, and sandals. Her makeup was minimal, and her eyes were red, as if she'd been crying.

"We're friends," Delia said. "You're always welcome to come by anytime." She touched Avery's arm and urged her to take the empty seat on the couch next to Myrna.

"Thanks," Avery said.

"Can I get you something to drink?" Delia asked, then pointed at the box on the table. "We also have some cheesecake if you're hungry."

"No, I'm good," Avery said. "I wasn't planning on staying long. I was hoping…" She paused to inhale a deep breath. "Brady finally got his life together, and I'd hate to see Derek ruin it a second time." Her words came out raspy.

"What do you mean when you say 'ruin'?" I asked. We

couldn't help if we didn't know all the details, no matter how bad or painfully private they might be.

"He had a few scrapes with the law when he was younger. He never ended up in jail, but I'm afraid because of his past, the police will give him a hard time." She sniffed, appearing to be on the verge of crying. "I want to do something but have no idea where to start." She twisted her hands in her lap. "I've heard about that sleuthing thing you all do, and I thought you might be willing to help prove Brady's innocent."

Delia reached over and patted Avery's arm. "Of course, we'll do whatever we can. Won't we?" She looked to the rest of us for confirmation.

Even if Brady wasn't a suspect in Derek's murder, Delia, Myrna, and Vincent wouldn't pass on the opportunity to investigate, which meant I wouldn't either. When I first discovered that they got involved with solving crimes, I tagged along to make sure they didn't get in trouble. Now, my curiosity and determination to solve a mystery equaled theirs. "Absolutely," I said.

Myrna, Vincent, and Zoey also agreed.

"Has Carson accused him of anything?" I asked.

Avery rubbed her temples. "No...but—"

"You're afraid it will only be a matter of time before he does," I finished for her.

"Yes." She returned her hands to her lap and slumped her shoulders.

"How well do you know Ivy and Derek?" I asked. Avery had lived in the area longer than I had, and because her job required coordinating numerous community events, she knew a lot of the locals. Now that I knew she'd come from the same town as Ivy and Derek, she might be able to provide us with useful information, things none of the local gossip or research would uncover.

"We all grew up together in Clarksburry," Avery said. "Ivy and I didn't hang out with the same crowd. I knew her through Brady and thought she was a good person. I didn't think much of Derek because he always got Brady into trouble." She frowned. "Derek and Brady used to be close. He refused to tell me what happened to cause their falling out. Brady's a loyal friend, so it must have been something pretty bad. I was glad to hear Ivy finally came to her senses and got away from him."

"Do you know what caused their breakup?" I asked.

Avery shook her head. "Not really, though I'd heard rumors about them having money problems."

"Is there anything else you can think of that might help us find out who did this?" I asked.

"No," Avery said, getting to her feet. "If I hear anything else, I'll let you know."

After reassuring Avery that we'd do whatever we could to help her brother, Delia showed her to the door. I waited for Delia to return, then said, "I've been giving what I saw at the crime scene some thought. Do we all agree Derek's death was planned, possibly by someone he knew?"

Vincent was the first to comment. "Pulling the stake from the ground and removing the rope to the net took a little time. And some forethought."

"Then there's the to-go cup, which had to be a frame-up job," Myrna said.

"Whoever it was, had to get close enough to stab him in the chest," Delia said. "So, yes, there's a good chance Derek knew his killer."

"Okay then," Zoey said, hopping up and heading for the whiteboard. After uncapping a marker, she used it to write the word "Suspects" at the top of the board, then faced the group and asked, "Who do you guys want to include?"

"I guess we should start with Ivy and Brady," I said.

"I thought we agreed that they were innocent," Zoey said.

"Yes, but the first rule of sleuthing is to make sure everyone involved has an alibi," Vincent said.

"Got it." Zoey turned and wrote their names on the

board. She held her marker poised and glanced over her shoulder. "Next."

"I think we should include Natalie," Myrna said. "I know she was only Derek's girlfriend, not his wife, but I think she qualifies as a person of interest, don't you?"

It irritated me that Natalie had accused Brady of the murder and was going out of her way to ensure everyone thought he was guilty. "Very much so," I said.

"Absolutely," Delia said. "If for no other reason than to find out why she's so adamant Brady is responsible."

"What about Melanie?" I looked at Delia. "I know she's your friend, but I got the impression she didn't like Derek or the fact that he was dating her daughter."

"I wouldn't say we're friends, more like acquaintances," Delia said. "The only time she gives me more than a greeting is when we're working on the committee."

"Fair enough," I said, nodding at Zoey. "Go ahead and add both of them to the list."

"Do you think we should add Jacob?" Zoey asked.

"That's not a bad idea," I said. "We can't rule out jealousy." Which happened to be one of the top reasons for unnatural deaths.

"It sounds like there weren't many people who cared for Derek," I said, though I didn't think not liking someone was a good enough motive for murder. I'd learned from playing our mystery game that something else was always powering the drive to end a life. "Maybe once we start talking to people, we'll get a better sense of who hated him enough to kill him."

"Maybe we'll uncover a hidden secret," Myrna said, rubbing her hands together. "Maybe something dark and dangerous."

Vincent grunted. "I doubt the man was into espionage."

"You don't know that for sure," Myrna huffed.

Before their banter led to a discussion about whether or not Derek was a spy, I asked, "Vincent, do you suppose you could find out any information about Derek's new business?"

I wasn't surprised when he rolled his eyes and snorted. He'd been a computer engineer before he retired and stayed active by researching topics that wouldn't interest most people. Vincent was also good at uncovering data.

"It might be a good idea to find out why he'd chosen to relocate here," Delia said. "I'd think it would've been more lucrative to open a business in his hometown where everybody knew him."

My aunt was on to something. "Maybe he didn't have a good reputation with the townsfolk." So far, I could think of several people who'd voiced their dislike for the man. Were there more we didn't know about?

"He had to know Ivy was living here," Myrna said. "Do you think that had something to do with his choice?"

"I think it's definitely worth checking out," I said.

"If Derek wasn't popular in Clarksburry, then it's possible he'd made some enemies here too," Delia said.

"I agree," Myrna said, nodding. "I think I'll check with the network at the Promenade and see if anyone has heard anything juicy."

Her efforts might be wasted since Derek most likely didn't associate with anyone from the older crowd. I didn't like relying on gossip, but every now and then, Myrna learned something useful. "It couldn't hurt," I said, then realized I should've asked Avery if Derek had attended any of her events. If he had, it would've been nice to know who he hung out with.

"I think the first thing we need to do is stop by Sharpe's shop when Ivy is working and see if we can get her to give us more details about her relationship with Derek," I said.

"We should ask her about Brady as well," Delia said. "To see if there's more than a friend connection."

"I agree." The more insight we had, the better. Provided Ivy was willing to share with us the next time we spoke. "Natalie mentioned something about Ivy living with her brother," I said. "Maybe we should chat with him as well, get his perspective on things."

Relatives sometimes had a biased view, depending on their relationship with their family. Even so, it would be nice to know how Ivy's brother felt about Derek.

"Ivy might also be able to tell us if Derek had any enemies, ones we don't know about." I glanced at the whiteboard. Other than the scenarios provided by our online game, this was the first time we had an ample amount of names. I hoped our talk with Ivy uncovered some clues, but I also hoped it didn't supply us with additional suspects.

The hard part would be tracking everyone down without appearing suspicious or drawing Carson's attention. Brady would be the easiest to contact since he maintained Delia's lawn and outside plants. I didn't keep track of his schedule, but my aunt did. "When is Brady due to work on your yard again?"

Her grin told me I didn't need to explain my reason for asking. "The day after tomorrow. He usually shows up between two-thirty and three in the afternoon."

"Good," I said. "If I hurry with closing chores, I should be able to make it home before he arrives without any problems."

CHAPTER EIGHT

After my shift at the Bean, Delia and I, under the guise of taking a late lunch, showed up at Sharpe's Sandwich and Snacks. I'd thought about calling first to see if Ivy was working but was afraid she might recognize my voice. Even if she wasn't there, I wouldn't view it as a wasted trip, not when I got to spend time with my aunt.

The area of town where the store was located wasn't within walking distance from Delia's home, so we had to drive. It was a part of town I hadn't seen yet. The main street was similar to the one near Archer's place. Only there were fewer shops and more professional businesses.

We'd timed our visit well. There weren't any other customers in the place, which would make asking Ivy questions easier. I peered through the glass door and saw her standing behind a serving counter near the back wall, talking to another woman, their discussion less than friendly. As soon as Delia and I entered, we remained quiet and stayed near the front door, hoping to overhear something useful before they noticed us.

The woman next to Ivy slapped her hands on her hips and snapped, "I told James helping you out was going to bring us nothing but trouble. Even dead, he's causing

65

problems. We'll never recoup the money we would've made from the stuff on the cart now that the police won't let us remove it from their crime scene."

Ivy straightened her shoulders. "It's not like I asked Derek to follow me here. And I certainly didn't ask someone to kill him."

"Are you sure?" the woman asked. "People are saying you got your new boyfriend to do it for you." The woman must've been talking about Brady, but I had yet to confirm that he and Ivy were actually dating.

Ivy groaned. "I've already told you we're just friends."

"Whatever." The woman dismissed Ivy with a wave of her hand, then smacked her palm on the door marked for employees only before slipping past it.

"Seriously," Ivy said in a heightened voice. "You need to stop listening to what other people say." She blew out an exasperated breath, dropping her head back and staring at the ceiling.

So far, she hadn't seen us, so I cleared my throat and said, "Good afternoon, Ivy."

She jerked her head in our direction, red spreading across her cheeks. "Oh, hey, Brinley, Delia." Ivy glanced at the swinging door behind her. "You heard that, didn't you?"

I walked toward her. "It was kind of hard to miss."

"I'm so sorry." Ivy released a nervous laugh. "That's the second time you've had to witness my chaotic life."

I could relate to how she was feeling. A future-changing disruption to my own life had prompted my relocation. "I don't think there's anyone on the planet who can say their life is perfect," I said, hoping to alleviate her embarrassment.

Ivy chuckled. "You could be right. I wouldn't mind a few hours of serenity, though I doubt I'll get some anytime soon." She flicked her wrist at the closed door leading to the back of the building. "Do you remember me mentioning my brother's wife, Amelia?" she asked in a lowered voice.

I nodded.

"Well, that was her."

"Oh," I mumbled since I couldn't think of anything appropriate to say. Ivy's harpy comment flashed through my mind. After witnessing the woman's rude outburst, I could think of a few other descriptive words that applied.

Amelia clearly disliked Derek. Would that have been enough of a reason to end his life? She seemed unapproachable, so finding a way to ask her questions would be difficult. It was a dilemma I'd share once Delia and I regrouped with the others.

"Anyway, she doesn't like me very much, and most of the time, I ignore her. She's not quite so bad when James is around." Ivy leaned on the counter. "I've only been staying with them a few months, and during that time, he's gotten good at running interference."

"She seemed pretty upset when we came in," Delia said.

"Yeah." Ivy sighed. "She thinks Derek's death is going to somehow ruin the shop's reputation."

"Why would she think that?" I asked.

"Because he's my ex and because I found the body, which happened to be next to *their* food trailer," Ivy said sarcastically.

"Neither of those things was your fault," I said.

Ivy shrugged. "I know, but with Amelia, everything's guilt by association. If I was going to get rid of Derek, which I didn't, I would've done it a long time ago. And,"—she drew out the word—"I certainly wouldn't have left him lying around for someone to find so easily."

I couldn't fault Ivy for dreaming up ways to get rid of her ex. Stacy and I had never been in a relationship, but I'd been guilty of contemplating her demise once or twice. She'd started dating a guy I'd gone out with a few times when I'd first moved to the city. Rick and I had been friends, nothing more, but it hadn't stopped her from viewing me as competition.

The management promotion I'd been promised to replace my boss when he retired had turned into an offer of relocation to another office in Minnesota. I was a sunshine and beaches kind of girl who had no interest in dealing with cold weather. Having to wear parkas and boots, or shoveling snow off sidewalks, was not the future I'd planned for myself.

The next part of our conversation would get more personal, and I didn't want anyone to overhear us. I shifted sideways and leaned against the counter so I could watch the main entrance and the door Amelia had disappeared behind at the same time. "Do you have any idea who might have wanted Derek dead?" I asked.

"No," Ivy said.

"How about enemies? Does anyone specific come to mind?"

Ivy chuckled. "That's a pretty long list. Up until the day of the game, I didn't even know he was in town."

"Do you think someone from Clarksburry could've followed him here?" Delia asked.

"Anything's possible, I guess," Ivy said. "Derek did some shady things back home that upset quite a few people, including me. I wouldn't be surprised if he'd already crossed more than one person here."

"If you don't mind, could you elaborate on what you consider 'shady?' I asked.

Ivy bit her lower lip, and I feared I'd gotten too intrusive. "With Derek, it was always about acquiring money," she said. "I can't tell you how many get-rich-quick schemes he had going. None of them worked, and they all involved someone else's bankroll."

I shot Delia a sidelong glance. Had we uncovered a possible motive for Derek's murder?

"Was that all you needed?" Ivy asked, apparently done answering any more questions.

"We actually stopped by for lunch," Delia said.

"And a couple of those wonderful cookies I had at the game," I said. "Provided you have any left."

Ivy giggled. "You're in luck. I made a fresh batch this morning." She waved her hand at the menu posted on the wall behind her. "I'll give you a minute to decide what you want. Unless you're ready to order now."

Since Delia had been to the shop a few times, she already knew what she wanted. After giving the menu a quick perusal, it didn't take me long to decide and place an order.

"Good choices. I'll have these ready for you in no time," Ivy said, then went to work preparing our food.

"Let's find a place to sit," Delia said as she headed for a table in the far corner near the front window. While we waited, Amelia peeked her head out, saw that we were the only customers, shot Ivy an I-told-you-so look, and disappeared into the back again.

Not long after Ivy delivered our order, her brother entered the shop. "I thought you were going to work out at the gym," she said.

"I am, but I forgot my bag," he said as he rounded the counter and disappeared into the back.

"Hey, Tate," Ivy said when the front door opened a second time. "I'd ask how it's going, but,"—she glanced at the medical boot on his foot—"it looks like you're still recovering."

We hadn't officially met, but I recognized Tate the second he hobbled further into the shop on his crutches. I hadn't seen him hanging around with Derek or Ivy at the game and hadn't realized they knew each other. Of course, I was still in the meeting people phase of the newest chapter in my life and relied on my aunt and friends to explain the town's dynamics.

Delia and I were sitting far enough away that we could have continued our conversation without being overheard if we kept our voices low. I was more interested in hearing what Tate and Ivy had to say and whether or not Derek's name came up in their conversation. My aunt raised a brow as she took a bite from her sandwich, letting me know she was doing the same thing.

"Yeah, and if I behave myself, I should be walking without these in no time." Tate winked and patted his crutches.

"We both know that's never going to happen." Ivy chuckled. "Since you're here, can I get you anything?"

"No, thanks," Tate said. "I'm not allowed to drive, so James is giving me a ride to the gym. We only stopped because—"

"He forgot his bag." Ivy hitched her thumb toward the door. "Again."

"Yep," Tate chuckled.

"Wait a second. How are you planning to work out with a messed up foot?"

"I can still exercise my upper body." Tate leaned on the crutches, then raised his arms and flexed his muscles. "You know, so I can impress the girls."

Ivy laughed. "Yeah, yeah, okay."

Loud voices echoed from the other side of the door. Delia and I were too far away to make out what was being said. Tate and Ivy didn't seem to have the same problem. "Sounds like Amelia's in one of her moods again," Tate said.

Ivy glanced over her shoulder and frowned. "When isn't she?"

"So, what's got her riled up today?"

"Believe it or not, Derek."

"Why? Does she think you're responsible for what happened to him?" Tate seemed uncomfortable and adjusted the position of his crutches.

People sensed things even if they didn't realize they were doing it. Being watched was one of them. If Tate looked in our direction, I didn't want to be caught staring and focused my attention on my sandwich.

Ivy sighed. "Supposedly, I'm somehow to blame

because she thinks his death will be bad for business."

"Well, that's ridiculous," he snarled.

"Especially since I didn't even know he was in town." Ivy crossed her arms and scowled. "But it seems you did since you played volleyball together. So why didn't you tell me?"

"Ivy, I can explain," Tate stammered.

I couldn't blame Ivy for being upset. I'd be mad too if people I considered friends kept something that important from me.

"It will have to wait because we need to go," James said as he pushed through the door carrying a bag. He didn't look happy, leaving me to believe the argument with his wife hadn't ended well.

"I'll see you later," he said, patting the top of his sister's head, then dodging her irritated swing as he rounded the counter.

I waited for James and Tate to leave, then asked Delia, "Have you ever met the guy who left with Ivy's brother?"

"No, have you?" Delia asked.

I took a drink of my tea, washing down the last bite of my sandwich. "Do you remember me telling you about the guy Jackson replaced in the game because he'd injured his foot?"

"Was that him?"

"Yes, and it sounds like he knew Derek."

"It's too bad James interrupted when he did. It would've been nice to know why Tate hadn't told Ivy her ex had moved here," Delia said, wiping her hands with her napkin, then placing it on her empty plate.

Though we kept our voices low, I didn't want Ivy to overhear our conversation, and glanced across the room to ensure she was occupied with something else. "I was thinking the same thing. If Tate knew Derek was in town, then there's a good chance James did too." I clicked my fingernails on the tabletop, contemplating. "If I'm right, what possible reason could he have for not telling his sister?"

"Maybe he thought he was protecting her," Delia said.

"Could be, but this town isn't that big. She would've found out eventually."

"That's true," Delia said, taking a bite of her cookie.

I silently relished the delectable taste of my own dessert and contemplated everything we'd learned. Once I'd polished off the second cookie, I pulled out my cell phone and checked the time. "It's not too late to stop by Leona's shop and see if she's heard anything interesting about Derek."

"I'm in," Delia said, draining the last of her drink.

"I think we should see if Myrna wants to tag along," I said, retrieving my phone and tapping her speed dial number.

It took five rings, and Myrna sounded winded when she finally answered.

"Hey, Myrna," I said. "Does Ziggy need anything?"

"Why?" she asked, suspicion lacing her voice.

"Delia and I finished having lunch at Sharpe's and were heading over to the boutique. We wondered if you want to go along," I said.

"No, he's good, but thanks for asking," Myrna said. "While you're getting the scoop from Leona, I think I'll pop over to the Promenade and check in with my resources." When she paused, it sounded like she was drinking something. "How did it go with Ivy?"

"I think it went well," I said. "Rather than fill you in on the phone, why don't we regroup with Vincent later and compare notes."

"It's a plan. I'll talk to you soon." Myrna said, then disconnected the call.

CHAPTER NINE

Delia and I arrived at Pemshaw's Pet Boutique thirty minutes before closing. Leona was cuddling a fluffy white Pomeranian against her chest and talking to a customer when we entered her shop. Even though she wasn't a natural blonde, the color and shoulder-length style of her hair was professionally done. All her employees wore a similar version of her uniform; a pair of black pants and a pink top that zipped along the front and had large pockets below the waist.

Her place reminded me of a salon for pets. Half of the interior was designed to handle all types of grooming needs, which included haircuts, bathing, and nail trimming. The other half hosted a decent variety of supplies for all types of critters. She even had a wall lined with tanks containing saltwater and freshwater fish.

Harley loved the place, and I felt bad for not bringing him with us. Delia had taken him for a short walk before we went to lunch, so I knew we wouldn't have any accidents by the time we got back to her place.

As soon as she saw us, Leona waved, then signaled one of her workers to take the dog she was holding. Rachel Botkin, another of Leona's employees, reached us before she did. She was in her early twenties and had a bounce in her step that caused the long, dark brown strands in her ponytail to sway back and forth. Her eye makeup was an artful combination of bold colors in different shades, something she changed every time I saw her.

"You poor thing," Rachel said, pulling me into a hug without bothering to greet me first. "Are you doing all right?"

Rachel hadn't worked at the shop long. She was always helpful and, at times, overly exuberant. I didn't think the few times we'd interacted had reached the comfortable hugging level yet, but I didn't say anything because I didn't want to hurt her feelings. "Fine," I said, stepping back when she released me. "Why?"

"I heard you were at the beach when they found that guy's body," she said. "This is the second one since you moved here, and I was worried you might develop some kind of stress disorder. Maybe be afraid to go on the beach ever again. Which would be horrible because, you know, Hawkins Harbor is a *beach* town."

"Actually, Ivy Sharpe's the one who found him," I said. "I happened to be in the area because I was taking Harley for a walk."

"Oh, good," Rachel said. "I'm glad to hear it because I had a cousin who found a dead lizard in her backyard when she was a kid, and she still cringes whenever she walks on the grass."

I didn't want to minimize her cousin's phobia by telling her that finding a lizard carcass was a lot different than discovering a dead body. Luckily, Leona put an end to the awkward conversation. "Rachel, don't you have some work you need to finish before we close?"

"Yeah. Right…I'm on it," Rachel said, then hustled to the other side of the room.

"Sorry about that," Leona said. "Rachel's a great worker, and the customers love her, but she can be a little…"

I dismissed the interaction by flicking my wrist. "It's okay. She's young and will eventually grow out of it." Or so I hoped.

Leona flashed me a look that said she didn't believe it any more than I did. "Rachel did make a good point, though."

"What would that be?" I asked.

"You've been involved in finding two bodies since you moved here," Leona said. "Not only is it unusual, but I'm hoping it doesn't influence your opinion of our town." She glanced at Delia. "We like having you here."

I draped my arm across my aunt's shoulders, and in case she needed one, I gave her a reassuring squeeze. "I like being here too, and I'm not going anywhere."

"Great." Leona clapped her hands together. She leaned closer and lowered her voice. "Did you see anything interesting at the crime scene?"

I'd seen plenty, but I wasn't willing to share any of the details with Leona. She liked to gossip, and I was afraid anything I told her would reach the wrong ears. Mainly Carson's.

I started with facts I was fairly certain Leona had already heard. "We spoke with Avery, and she's worried about her brother," I said. "It seems Natalie is going around town telling everyone that Brady's responsible for Derek's death."

"I've already heard something similar from several of my customers," Leona said, scowling. "Natalie has been a troublemaker for as long as I've known her. She won't stop spreading rumors until the police find the real killer."

It was pretty much the same thing Zoey told us during her rant about Natalie. What worried me was how the town's residents would react or how they'd treat Brady afterward. Would he end up losing his lawn maintenance work because of Natalie's irresponsible behavior? I planned to ask him how things were going and see if I could extract additional information about his relationship with Derek when he came by to work on Delia's lawn.

Carson was good at his job, but it didn't mean he'd be able to find out who'd ended Derek's life overnight. The more I worried about what would happen to Brady in the interim, the more determined I was to solve the crime.

"I didn't know Derek, did you?" Delia asked.

Leona tucked her hands in her pockets. "I'm afraid not. I didn't even know Ivy had been married to him until I ran into her sister-in-law Amelia."

After seeing Amelia in person, I could only imagine what she'd had to say. "Did Amelia have any opinions about Derek's death?"

Leona snickered. "Plenty."

"Really, like what?" I asked, hoping to hear something new.

Leona frowned. "Mostly that they'll suffer a drop in business because Derek was Ivy's ex."

"Do you know why James and Amelia started a business here instead of in Clarksburry?" I asked, assuming that all the Sharpes had relocated to Hawkins Harbor.

"Amelia actually grew up here," Leona said. "I'm not sure how she and James got together, but I do know she refused to move after they got engaged. Coastal towns draw more tourists, so their business probably does better here than it would've in Clarksburry, which is quite a bit smaller."

The front door opened, drawing Leona's gaze to the middle-aged woman entering the shop. "I..." Leona took a hesitant step, then stopped when Rachel went to greet their newest customer. "Never mind." Leona widened her eyes as if remembering something important. "Oh, before I forget. We received a new shipment of fish earlier this afternoon. I'd planned to call but got sidetracked with a grooming emergency."

After Herman, one of the fish who'd been a longtime resident in the shop's aquarium, went belly up, I'd been checking the tanks at the boutique to find a replacement.

Besides wanting to surprise Zoey and Archer with a replacement, I was curious to find out if Zoey would call the fish Herman the second or if she'd give him a new name altogether.

Leona motioned for Delia and me to follow her to the wall lined with tanks. There were actually three vibrant blue fish in the same aquarium. "These are perfect." I studied them as they swam around, trying to decide which one to pick. "It's hard to decide."

I wanted to get the healthiest one of the bunch that closely resembled Herman.

"I rather like the big one in the back," Delia said, pointing at her selection.

I smiled at Leona. "I guess we'll take that one."

CHAPTER TEN

Per the instructions I'd received from Leona, I couldn't leave the fish I'd purchased in the bag overnight without risking his demise. The Bean had been closed for hours, but being the manager meant I had a key to the building. The sun hadn't set, and there was still plenty of light for me to take a trip to the coffee shop and walk Harley at the same time before it was too dark to see where I was going.

When we reached the shop, Harley and I made our way to the back of the building. I hadn't expected to see Quincy hanging around waiting to be fed, but I scanned the area anyway. On my days off, Archer put food out for the cat. Though, I didn't think he spent any time trying to befriend him.

There weren't any windows near the exit, so once inside, I switched on the interior light, then secured the door's lock behind us. "I can't let you run around the food area, so I'm afraid you have to stay in here until I'm done," I told Harley after leading him into the office and unclipping his leash.

My dog fared pretty well when left on his own. There wasn't anything in the room he could damage. I'd expected some whimpering, maybe even barking, and was glad when he started exploring and sniffing everything he could reach with his nose.

Leona's instructions had been easy to remember, but even if I'd forgotten what she told me, I could always use the bullet-point list printed on the outside of the plastic bag. I lifted the lid on top of the aquarium and gently set the bag in the water. Waiting for the water in the bag to match the tank's temperature was an essential part of acclimating the fish to his new home.

After setting the timer on my cell phone, I sat at the counter to keep an eye on my new acquisition. Watching the rest of the colorful fish swim through the water was calming and mesmerizing. It didn't take long before my thoughts drifted to Derek's death or for me to wonder what he'd done to provoke someone into murdering him.

Because of the stake in his chest and Brady's discarded to-go cup at the crime scene, I was still going with the theory that his murder had been preplanned. Greed was always a good motivator, but I didn't have enough information to know if money was the driving force behind his demise or if it had been something else entirely. The only way my friends and I would find a reason was by talking to people who knew him. I had a feeling the list we'd comprised might be incomplete.

I had no doubt some of the residents in Clarksburry would be able to supply pertinent information. Unfortunately, I didn't know any of the residents and didn't have a clue where to start looking for answers.

When the melodic chime for the timer on my phone went off, it made me jump and pulled me from my troubling thoughts. I hopped off my seat and rounded the counter. "Okay, Herman number two," I said, making a hole in the end of the bag and releasing the pocket of air. "Are you ready to check out your new home?"

I hadn't expected an answer but was happy to see the fish swim through the hole. I replaced the tank's hood, then watched him for several more minutes, looking for signs of distress. Convinced the transition had gone well, I went to collect my dog.

It didn't take long to turn off the lights, lock up, and be on our way. Harley and I had barely reached the side of the building when he started barking at someone emerging from the front. Recognizing Douglas came too late to stop my scream that sounded more like a shrill squeak.

He was dressed in his police uniform, so he was either on his way home or working. I believed it was the latter since he didn't live in Delia's neighborhood, and the only other residential area was on the opposite side of the nearest parking lot.

It took a few seconds for the pounding in my chest to ease. "What are you doing out here lurking in the shadows?" I asked, giving Douglas a stern look.

"I wasn't hiding, I promise." Embarrassed, he tucked his chin and stuck his hands in his pockets. Before I could chastise him further, he hurried to add, "I saw the light on inside the Bean and thought someone had broken in."

I refrained from pointing out that thieves, specifically those who were any good and afraid they'd get caught, didn't turn on interior lights. "I'm sure Archer will appreciate hearing that you were looking out for his place."

"Thanks," he said. "Would you mind telling me why you were here after hours?"

"I bought a new fish at the pet boutique and stopped to put him in the aquarium."

"Good call," Douglas said.

"I thought so." I grinned, glad he knew something about acclimating fish from one tank to another and wouldn't ask for an explanation.

We shared a brief moment of uncomfortable silence before Douglas spoke again. "You shouldn't be out here walking alone... Not after what happened."

"I'm not alone. I brought my guard dog with me," I said, smiling down at Harley, who wasn't vicious and had a sweet personality. He was more likely to overtake somebody with doggy kisses than a bite to the ankle.

Douglas rolled his eyes. "Yeah, he looks like he could do a lot of damage if provoked."

I quirked a brow. "Are you trying to tell me we might have a serial killer stalking the beach?" The odds of me running into teenagers sneaking onto the beach after dark to party or make out was a lot higher than encountering someone looking to do harm to others.

"No, that's not what I'm saying. I think it would be wise not to take walks alone until we find the killer."

"You're out here by *yourself*." I placed my free hand on my hip. "If you're right, then there's a good chance the killer won't care if you're in law enforcement."

He chuckled. "I guess you have a point."

Now that I had him away from Carson's watchful eye, I wanted to see if he'd divulge some information about Derek's murder.

"Did you know Derek?" I asked.

"Not personally. I work out at Haskell's Gym a few times a week and remember seeing him there several times."

If Derek worked out at the gym, maybe he'd made a friend or two. Or possibly an enemy, given that he was now deceased. Visiting the gym sounded like a good place to start, but I didn't want to go without knowing what to expect first. "I've never been to a gym before."

"You should give it a try," Douglas said. "Not that I think you're in need of a workout or anything." He glanced at the ground, nervously shifting from one foot to another.

"Do you need to be a member to attend?" I asked, pretending not to notice his discomfort.

"I do." He raised his gaze and grinned. "I think they'll give you a tour if you ask."

"Does Carson also go there to work out?" The man was in great shape. I wouldn't be surprised if he did. I was more concerned about running into him and what he'd do if he happened to catch my friends and me questioning people about Derek.

"No," Douglas said. "He prefers running and outdoor sports to stay in shape."

Good to know.

Whether Douglas knew it or not, he'd provided me with another clue. He seemed less guarded, so maybe I could extract more information. "I'm not an expert or anything, but what I saw of the crime scene makes me think the death was personal," I said.

I feigned a shudder. "Do you think it was a crime of passion?" I hoped to distract Douglas before he told me he couldn't discuss an ongoing investigation. "I can understand a woman being filled with rage, but would they be strong enough to stab a man in the chest like that?"

Douglas shrugged. "You'd be surprised what someone can do if they're angry enough."

Actually, I wouldn't. Because of my weekly online mystery game sessions, I'd played through enough scenarios to know anything was possible.

Harley tugged his leash, letting me know he was tired of staying in one place and needed to take care of business. "We should get going. Delia's expecting us home soon."

"Do you want me to escort you to her house?" Douglas asked.

I took a few steps backward, letting Harley lead. "I'm sure we'll be fine, but thanks."

"Holler if you see anything suspicious."

"Will do," I called, waving goodbye as I turned.

CHAPTER ELEVEN

As soon as I reached Delia's house, she informed me that we'd been invited to Vincent's place for dinner. My aunt's place had a great ocean view, but I enjoyed spending time in Vincent's backyard. The awning covering his concrete patio extended far enough away from the house to protect his grill from the weather.

The rest of his yard was covered in freshly mowed, lush green grass and a couple of small, randomly placed trees. He had six-foot hedges running along both sides of his property that looked as if they'd been recently trimmed. According to Vincent, the squared-off shrubs provided a natural fence and ensured his privacy from nosy neighbors.

Harley also enjoyed the outing. Most of his time was spent exploring. The remainder was spent under the patio table while we ate, watching for escaping tidbits of food.

Vincent was the only one of us who didn't own a pet. According to him, a mishap with a fish as a child was enough trauma to keep him from graduating to anything with four legs. It didn't stop him from encouraging me to bring Harley along for our visits.

Being a pro at preparing meals on his grill was another reason I looked forward to gathering at his house.

Tonight's entree was chicken breasts basted in barbecue sauce, a special recipe Vincent made from scratch.

He owned several aprons and liked to wear one when he cooked. My favorite was dark green and had a dancing hamburger on the front, though the orange one he was wearing came in second because of the hot dog made to look like a cute Dachshund printed on the bib.

After setting places for dinner, we'd each grabbed a glass of tea and were lounging in seats around the table. "Did you learn anything useful from Leona?" Vincent asked as he flipped the meat with metal tongs, then coated each piece with another layer of sauce.

I took a sip, then set my glass on the table. "Not really," I said. "She basically told us the same thing Zoey had about Natalie and the rumors she's been spreading about Brady offing Derek."

"Well, darn," Myrna groaned and pushed her glasses up her nose. "She usually has the best information."

"Leona did say that she's never met Derek or heard anyone mention him before he was murdered," Delia added. "She didn't know he was Ivy's ex either until Amelia Sharpe told her after his body had been found."

"Did Leona learn anything else from Amelia," Vincent asked.

"Only that she's convinced Derek's murder will ruin their business," I said.

"No surprise there," Myrna said. "That woman spends all her time complaining. The only reason their shop stays in business is because of James and the great food they serve."

"How about you?" I asked Myrna. "Did you hear any good gossip from the network?"

Myrna sighed. "Nothing we didn't already know."

"On the upside," Delia said. "Leona got in a new shipment of fish, and Brinley found a replacement for Herman."

Myrna widened her eyes. "You didn't leave him alone

with Luna, did you?" She sounded as if I'd committed an unthinkable act.

When I'd planned for the fish's welfare, I hadn't even considered the possibility of the little critter becoming an appetizer for Delia's cat. "Of course not. I took him to the Bean and settled him into his new home."

Relieved, Myrna slumped back in her seat. "Did he adjust okay?"

"He seemed to be doing all right when I left," I said. "You can check him out for yourself in the morning." Knowing Myrna, she'd probably arrive earlier than normal for her daily breakfast with Delia and Vincent to see how the new fish was doing.

"I might have discovered a new clue," I said.

"Really?" Delia asked.

I'd decided to wait until we were all together before telling my aunt about my talk with Douglas. "I ran into officer Dankworth outside of the Bean," I said.

"What was he doing over there?" Vincent asked.

"I think he was working," I said.

"What makes you think that?" Delia asked.

"He was wearing his uniform and made it sound like he was patrolling the beach." I remembered our conversation and grinned. "He was adamant about letting me know that I shouldn't be out walking alone."

"Do the police think there's a serial killer on the loose?" Myrna asked.

I found it amusing that her thoughts mirrored mine and chuckled. "I asked him the same thing, but he denied it. Maybe Carson's getting pressure from the sheriff since this is the second body found on a beach in the last few months."

Delia snorted. "I wouldn't doubt it." Landon Lennox wasn't one of her favorite people. I wasn't surprised by her disgusted tone or soured expression.

Myrna had shared her dislike for the man on numerous occasions. Vincent must've sensed an upcoming rant and changed the subject. "Brinley, you mentioned a new clue."

"I did," I said, acknowledging his foresight with a slight dip of my chin. "When I asked Douglas if he knew Derek before his death, he told me he'd seen him during workouts at Haskell's Gym."

"Ivy's brother James was on his way to a gym when we stopped by Sharpe's," Delia said. "Do you think he was going to the same place?"

"It would be a heck of a coincidence if he did," Myrna said.

When it came to mysteries, specifically those involving murder, none of us believed in coincidences. It would be easy to verify how many gyms the town had with a quick online search. My guess would be not very many. "If it is the same place, what do you think the odds are that James also ran into Derek while he was there?"

"I'd say they were decent," Vincent said. Having been an engineer, he viewed things analytically. He'd probably already done a statistical calculation in his mind.

"Didn't Ivy tell us she had no idea Derek had moved to town?" Delia asked.

"Yes," I said.

Delia furrowed her brows. "I didn't get the impression that she was lying, did you?"

I shook my head. Unless Ivy was a good actress, I struggled to believe she hadn't been truthful. "Some siblings can be overprotective. Maybe James knew and purposely didn't tell her." Maybe James wanted to protect his sister and handle Derek himself. Perhaps the fading bruise I'd glimpsed on Derek's face had been caused by her brother's fist and not a volleyball.

"I suppose it's possible," Delia said.

"And something we should check out," Myrna said.

"Which means we'll have to figure out a tactful way to question James when Amelia's not around," I said.

"At some point, I think we should also talk to Amelia," Delia said.

Even though I knew she was right, I still dreaded having to deal with the rude woman. "Unless an opportunity presents itself ahead of time, I'm okay with questioning Amelia last."

"Agreed," Myrna said, smirking.

"Dinner is almost ready," Vincent said as he picked up a piece of chicken and set it on a nearby plate. "Why don't we take a break and eat, then we can strategize a game plan."

The aroma coming from the grill made my mouth water and had my stomach making noises. "That definitely works for me."

CHAPTER TWELVE

As I'd predicted, Myrna showed up ten minutes early for her long-standing breakfast with Delia and Vincent so she could inspect our new fish. She'd joined Zoey and Archer in complimenting my selection. I'd been a little worried about the transition and was happy to see that Herman's replacement had survived the night and was swimming happily with the other inhabitants sharing the tank.

Zoey thought it might be bad luck to use the same name and had volunteered to come up with a new one but needed a day or two to think about it. It was one less task I had to worry about, and was fine with me.

The Bean was busier than usual, and the day passed quickly. Derek's death was all any of the regulars wanted to talk about. I didn't participate in sharing my views, but I wasn't opposed to hearing what others thought. Mainly because I'd hoped to glean some new clues.

Since Zoey was an honorary member of our mystery-solving group, I noticed her paying attention more than usual. She cringed every time someone mentioned Brady's name, and I didn't have to ask to know she was formulating ways to get back at Natalie.

Not that I could blame her. I'd had similar imaginings myself. Purposely accusing someone of a horrendous crime when there was a good chance they were innocent was despicable. Zoey wasn't vindictive, and I knew she had a good heart and wouldn't act on the impulse.

Cleaning up after closing took a little longer than normal, so I had to forgo stopping to enjoy viewing the ocean on my walk back to Delia's place. I arrived minutes before Brady parked his truck on the street in front of her house. I opened the door and hollered to let my aunt know I was home but wasn't worried when I didn't receive a reply. Harley came running, and after giving him a scratch behind the ear, I made him stay inside.

If Delia was upstairs and hadn't heard me, my dog's unhappy barking would bring her to the foyer in no time. We'd already discussed my plans to question Brady. She'd be able to watch us behind the blinds in the living room and had agreed to stay inside so I could talk to him alone. I figured since I wasn't technically a customer, he might be more inclined to answer my questions.

Brady was wearing a green, short-sleeved shirt with the logo for his business centered in large white letters across the front. The fabric fit snugly against the broad muscles of his chest. The exposed skin on his arms and legs was tanned from long hours spent working in the sun.

"Hey, Brinley," he said as he slid out of his truck.

"Hello back," I said. Other than occasionally running into each other and exchanging pleasantries, we'd never had any in-depth conversations, so I wouldn't classify us as friends. I had no idea how open he'd be if our conversation got more personal, but it didn't stop me from stepping off the porch and heading toward him. "How's your day going?" I decided to start out slow and see how things went before progressing to what I wanted to know.

"Not bad."

Delia's backyard consisted of a wooden deck with stairs that led down to the beach. The only plants that required care were the ones in the assortment of ceramic pots she'd arranged near the exterior of the house. Her front yard wasn't huge. The grass could be trimmed with a regular-sized mower, which was what Brady had strapped down in the vehicle's bed.

"I'm staying busy. And you?" He moved to the back of his truck and leaned over the frame. "Are you settling in okay?"

"Actually, I am," I said. "I like the town, and Archer's a great boss."

Brady was a handsome guy who liked to flirt with all the ladies. Myrna and Delia included. He flashed me a charming smile, which, if I'd been interested in him, would have made me blush.

"I'm glad you're here," Brady said as he hauled out a carryall containing trimming tools and set it on the sidewalk near his feet. "I wanted to thank you personally."

"For what?" I asked.

He pulled off his dark sunglasses and placed them on his head, his gaze turning serious. "For looking out for Ivy after she found Derek's body. She told me you took care of things so she wouldn't have to."

Most of the people in town probably knew it wasn't the first corpse I'd had to deal with, so I didn't need to remind him. "How's she doing?" She seemed to be handling things all right when Delia and I had stopped by the sandwich shop, but people were known to hide their true feelings in a professional setting.

"I think she'll be okay," Brady said. "She's tougher than she lets on."

I remembered how Ivy had stood up for herself with Amelia and figured he was right. "I'm glad to hear it." I took a moment to formulate how I should proceed. Brady cared about Ivy. How much was still unclear, so I had to be careful. If I asked the wrong thing or appeared to be pushy, he might refuse to answer my questions. "Am I right in assuming you knew Derek fairly well?"

Brady already knew Delia and I had overheard his heated conversation the day of the volleyball games, so I wasn't going to explain why I wanted to know unless he asked.

"We were friends...once."

"If you don't mind me asking, what happened to cause the change?" I used an encouraging tone, hoping he'd expound on their past relationship.

"I..." When he glanced at the ground and rubbed his nape, I was afraid he'd refuse to answer. "No, I don't mind. Now that he's dead, everyone's talking about what happened, and it won't take long before they find out anyway." He groaned. "Especially if Natalie doesn't stop bad-mouthing me."

"Yeah," I said. "I heard, and I'm really sorry."

He eyed me with a suspicious gaze. "Does that mean you don't think I did it, too?"

Instinctively, I thought he was innocent, but I still had unanswered questions and needed an alibi to rule him out completely. "I prefer not to base my decisions on what the local gossips have to say."

Brady smiled. "Fair enough." He leaned against the truck and propped an elbow on the bed frame. "I assume you and your friends are doing some of your behind-the-scenes sleuthing and have some questions."

"We are, and we do." I chuckled. There was a chance Brady might not appreciate his sister's interference, so I wasn't going to say anything about her request for help until he brought it up first.

"Ask away," he said.

"Did you know Derek had moved to town?" I asked, studying his expression, searching for signs that he was avoiding the truth.

"I found out a couple days before the volleyball event," Brady said.

"Why didn't you tell Ivy?"

"I was busy with jobs and didn't want to do it over the

phone. I figured I could get her alone at the game and planned to tell her then. Only Derek showed up with Natalie and beat me to it."

"Do you have any idea why he moved here?" I was leery about believing anything Natalie had to say, but there was a chance she was right about the money thing.

"I've been wondering that myself," Brady said, tapping the metal frame with his fingertips. "At first, I thought it might be because of Ivy."

"I take it he wasn't happy about the divorce," I said.

"Not from what I heard, but after seeing him with Natalie, it looks like he moved on," Brady said.

"So you think he was after something else."

"Yeah, and it most likely had to do with money."

My friends and I already had the financial angle on our list, but I was curious to glean more information. I raised a brow. "Why do you say that?"

"Derek possessed the charm of an experienced salesman," Brady said. "He could talk almost anyone into anything with very little effort."

"Including you?" I asked.

"Unfortunately, yes." Brady wrinkled his nose. "For a while anyway. Some of the things we did weren't exactly legal." I must've made a face because he quickly added, "It was petty stuff. I didn't go to jail, and I certainly didn't hurt or kill anyone." He sucked in a breath. "Though, if it wasn't for Avery, the jail thing might have actually happened. I'm not proud of what I did, but at the time, Derek convinced me we weren't doing anything wrong."

I wasn't about to judge because people made mistakes all the time, myself included. I had to give Brady credit for moving to a different place and starting over. It showed strength of character to learn from a bad experience and choose a better path.

I remembered Ivy's response to Derek's comment about starting a new business. I had no idea what she'd meant and needed clarity. "Do you think he was after Ivy's money?"

"No way." Brady's laugh sounded shallow. "Before the divorce, Derek ran up their bills and cleaned out their savings. Ivy was forced to start over. That's the main reason she moved here and is living with her brother James and his wife Amelia."

Ending up broke and having to live with relatives was a good motive for revenge, not necessarily murder. Ivy seemed to be handling her situation well. She hadn't seemed bitter when Delia and I spoke with her.

Derek had a girlfriend, so even if my suspicions about Brady having feelings for Ivy were correct, he had no reason to want her ex gone either.

"That must be difficult for her."

"You have no idea," Brady said.

After seeing how Amelia treated her sister-in-law firsthand, I was pretty sure I did.

He sighed. "I offered to help Ivy out, but she refused."

I could understand her wanting to be independent and having a place of her own. My circumstances were different. I was living with my aunt by choice, not because of a financial situation. If Delia had her way, she'd make me a permanent roommate. I had no intention of overstaying my welcome, and it wouldn't be long before I'd need to start looking for a place of my own.

"I appreciate your candor," I said since I didn't have any more questions.

"No problem."

"I'll let you get back to work." I headed for the house.

"Brinley," Brady called when I reached the porch.

"Yes," I said, glancing over my shoulder.

"Tell Delia and the gang thanks for me."

I smiled. "I will."

CHAPTER THIRTEEN

While we strategized at Vincent's home, he'd done a quick search on his computer and learned that Haskell's Gym was the only workout facility in town. It had to be where James and Tate were headed the day Delia and I had lunch at Sharpe's Sandwich Shop.

It also increased the odds that James knew Derek was in town. Though it was unlikely, there was always a chance their paths never crossed. Or that James wasn't the one who'd caused the bruise on Derek's face. Even if we asked James outright, I didn't think he'd admit to punching his sister's ex, not when it would make him look guilty for the man's murder.

The group unanimously agreed we needed to visit the gym to see if we could uncover anything new about Derek. Vincent had no interest in going, but as soon as we started discussing the trip, Myrna was more than happy to go along. I had a feeling it was because she was more interested in checking out men's muscles than sleuthing.

I'd never been to a gym before, and our main goal was to gather information. Even though the area had a large retiree community, it didn't necessarily mean the place had a lot of older members. I wanted to ensure we didn't attract unnecessary attention, which meant finding someone closer to my age to go with me.

After seeing Jackson play in the volleyball game, it was obvious he took care of his body. I'd thought about asking him to go, but I didn't know what he did to stay in shape or if he had a membership at the gym. Things between us were new, and I didn't want to risk changing the dynamics by asking him for a favor.

Fortunately, Zoey and I had gotten to be good friends. Her association with our mystery group made asking her for help much easier. Knowing that we were working to prove Brady's innocence and hopefully shut down Natalie's rampant gossip spree at the same time was a good motivator.

I agreed with her suggestion to dress appropriately for the outing. After a brief discussion on what that should be, we ended up with our hair pulled back in ponytails and similar outfits consisting of shorts, tank tops, and tennis shoes.

We'd both had to work, so instead of going home to change, we got ready at the shop. I also drove my car and left it in the lot not far from the Bean.

Haskell's Gym was located in an older area of town that I hadn't explored yet. The outside of the building was in good condition but looked as if it was overdue for a fresh coat of light-brown paint. A sign made of large individual letters done in white with a black trim filled the area above the awning running the length of the entire block.

I'd parked across the street and far enough away so we could easily observe the front of the business without being noticed.

"What's the game plan?" Zoey asked as she stared out the front window from the passenger seat of my car. Her excitement about being included in the group's newest excursion was evident in her beaming grin.

"Not letting anyone know what we're up to." I was still

nervous about running into Carson.

"Got it." She shifted her focus to me. "Anything else?"

"I have no idea who Derek interacted with, but hopefully, we'll find someone who knew him," I said, tapping the steering wheel. "If that happens, we'll have to play it by ear."

"Okay then," Zoey said, reaching for the door handle. "Let's go."

Even though it was late in the afternoon, the heat and humidity were still noticeable, and I enjoyed the blast of cool air we received as soon as we stepped inside.

A long counter filled a portion of the reception area. The company name was printed on the wall behind it.

I could see people operating some of the machines through the open doorway on the left, but didn't see anyone I recognized. To the right was a hallway that led to the back of the building. There wasn't an employee-only sign posted over the entryway, so I assumed it was open to the public.

Zoey was scanning the place as well. She had the advantage of knowing more of the locals, which made bringing her along a good choice.

An older man with hints of gray in his dark hair was standing behind the counter and looked up from whatever he was showing the younger man next to him. Judging by their appearance, I guessed the older guy to be somewhere in his forties, the younger in his mid to late twenties. They wore matching yellow T-shirts that sported the company logo and clung tightly to their chests, making it apparent they worked out regularly.

"Good afternoon, ladies. I'm Louis Haskell, the owner, but you can call me Lou."

"It's nice to meet you, Lou." I pressed a hand to my chest. "I'm Brinley, and this is Zoey."

Lou acknowledged us with a welcoming smile and a nod. "What can I do for you today?"

"We were interested in learning more about your

memberships," I said.

"Have you ever been to a gym before?" he asked.

"No," I said. "This is our first time." Some owners were curious about their marketing efforts, and I was afraid Lou might ask how we'd heard about his place. I couldn't risk news of our visit getting back to Douglas or Carson and had a not-quite-truthful alternative response ready to go.

"Great, Adam can give you a full tour." He patted the younger man's shoulder. "He can also answer any questions you may have about the place."

"My pleasure," Adam said, grinning. His amber eyes sparkled with the prospect of a new sale. "Right this way." He motioned us toward the room filled with equipment.

"Let me introduce you to one of our trainers," Adam said as he approached a man who had his back to us.

I was elated when Jacob, one of our possible suspects, turned to face us. With any luck, he'd be willing to answer my questions and maybe even supply a much-needed clue.

His surprise at seeing me transformed into a smile as soon as he saw Zoey. Instead of a T-shirt, he wore a black tank top with the gym's logo, which exposed more of his broad chest and some nicely defined arm muscles. The last time I'd seen him I'd been too distracted by Derek's death and his conversation with Natalie to pay much attention to his looks.

"Hey, Jacob," Zoey said. "I didn't know you were a personal trainer."

Jason puffed out his chest. "I got my certification a few months ago."

"That's awesome, congrats," she said, then, in an attempt to stall our tour, she added, "This is my friend, Brinley." Zoey swept her hand in my direction. "She recently moved here and works with me at the Bean."

"We've met. Well, sort of," Jacob said.

He was right. No one had actually introduced us during the time we'd spent near the beach waiting for the police to finish with their crime scene so we could leave.

Adam shot me a confused look. I didn't want to go into a lengthy explanation, so I nudged Zoey, then directed my gaze to a row of machines on the other side of the room.

Thankfully, she was quick to pick up my hint. "Adam," she said, flashing him a flirtatious smile. "I don't suppose we could take a look at the equipment over there." She pointed as she tucked her arm through his. "And maybe you can demonstrate how each one works."

"I'd be happy to," he said, glancing at me. "Are you coming with us?" I knew he was being polite, but his expression suggested otherwise.

I fought back a grin. "You go ahead. I'll catch up shortly. I'd like to chat with Jacob. That is if you don't mind." I quirked an inquiring brow, pretty sure he wouldn't refuse a potential customer's request.

"Not at all," he said, though he didn't sound very convincing.

I waited for Adam and Zoey to be out of earshot before speaking. "With everything that happened, I didn't get a chance to tell you how sorry I was about your friend Derek." I hoped expressing empathy would encourage him to talk.

"Who told you we were friends?" Jacob asked, scowling.

Judging by his reaction, I'd need to be careful with my words. When he'd arrived to console Natalie, we'd all been standing close together, so I couldn't be accused of eavesdropping. I knew I shouldn't feel guilty, but I did. "Natalie seemed to think you were close."

"Sometimes she gets things wrong," Jacob said, swiping his hand through his hair.

After hearing the accusations Natalie had made about Ivy and Brady, I'd already figured that much out for myself. "Oh," I said, feigning innocence.

"To be honest, I didn't like the guy. I only got along

with him because I knew it would upset Natalie if I didn't." He pressed his lips together, holding whatever he was about to say back, which I was fairly certain had to do with him still having feelings for her. Granted, she was a nice-looking woman, but I didn't see the appeal, not after she shared her views. Jacob obviously found something to like about her, so I kept my opinions to myself.

I wanted to clear Jacob from our suspect list and moved on to something a little more personal. "Was she the reason you were arguing with Derek during intermission at the volleyball game?" I used a softened tone, hoping I seemed sympathetic rather than nosy.

When Jacob crossed his arms, I wasn't sure he was going to answer. "Ivy's brother James is one of my clients, and he told me about Derek's penchant for making off with other people's money. I wanted to make sure he didn't do the same thing to Natalie and gave him a warning."

I thought about the faded yellowish-purple mark on Derek's face. Unless he'd been in a bar fight, which I highly doubted, the injury was most likely caused by a jealous suitor or family member. My instincts were still leaning toward James as the main candidate.

Derek already had the bruise when Jacob confronted him about the money, but it didn't mean it was their first argument. I needed to be sure. "Derek had the remnants of a bruise around his eye. Were you responsible?" I asked, closely watching his expression for any signs of guilt.

"I wish." Jacob sighed. "Derek most likely deserved it, but I have no idea how he got it or if someone punched him." He held up a hand. "And before you ask, I didn't kill him either. Sure, I would give anything to win Natalie back, but it has to be her choice, not because she's vulnerable and rebounding after losing Derek."

I glanced toward the area where Adam had taken Zoey. She wouldn't be able to keep him distracted for much longer. So far, Jacob had confirmed a few of my suspicions, but he hadn't provided me with any new clues. "I heard Derek was starting a business," I said. "Would you happen to know anything about it?"

Jacob shrugged. "If he was, he never said anything about it to me."

"Do you think he might have shared the details with Natalie?" If Derek was sly enough to charm people out of their money, he'd probably coerced Natalie into sharing details about her past, including her relationship with Jacob and any other people she knew. Approaching Jacob about a financial endeavor would be dangerous, but going after Natalie's friends seemed plausible.

"It's possible, but you'd have to ask her," he said.

Though I'd wanted to avoid it, deep down I knew talking to Natalie would be inevitable. I hoped the information my friends and I had gathered to date would be enough to help us through any half-truths she provided.

A young woman dressed in a sports bra and shorts appeared in the lobby and waved at Jacob. He lifted his index finger, signaling he'd be right with her. "My appointment's here, so I need to get back to work."

"I appreciate you taking the time to speak with me," I said.

"I'm not sure why you're interested in solving Derek's death," Jacob said. "I'd tell you to let the police handle it, but I get the impression it's somehow personal and you wouldn't heed my advice."

He didn't need to know that my friends and I were doing this for Avery and her brother. "You're right on both counts, but thanks anyway," I said, grinning.

Not long after Jacob walked away, Zoey and Adam joined me. "If you come with me, I'll show you the lockers and changing room."

I'd gotten the answers I wanted from Jacob and didn't need to see the rest of the building. I also didn't want to be rude to Adam. "Sure. Lead the way."

Zoey and I followed him through the lobby and down

the hallway I'd noticed earlier. He stopped after leading us past some bathrooms and into a room that had lockers lining two of the walls. There were also four closet-sized rooms with curtains pulled to the side for people who wanted privacy when they changed.

"Some of our members like to work out first thing in the morning before they head to work. "So we have showers in there," Adam said as he pointed toward the entrance to another room.

"That's convenient," I said.

Adam gave us a moment to look around. "I think that pretty much covers everything." He motioned toward the hallway.

The iced coffee I drank on the way to the gym had made its way through my system. My bladder picked that moment to let me know a trip to the bathroom was in order. "I hate to ask, but would you mind if I used the restroom before we leave?" I flashed him an embarrassed smile.

"Not a problem," Adam said. "We'll meet you up front."

I hurried off to take care of business. When I walked past the locker room on my way back, I heard a muffled voice coming from somewhere inside and thought Adam and Zoey had changed their minds about waiting for me in the lobby. Expecting to find them chatting about the showers, I stepped into the doorway and froze.

Instead of finding Adam and Zoey, I saw Tate pacing the floor and talking into his cell phone. "I'm working on it," he grumbled to whoever he was speaking with. "But I need more time."

He had a towel wrapped around his waist. His hair was wet, and water droplets glistened on his shoulders. His medical boot was sitting on the floor near a bench, his crutches propped against the nearby wall. What shocked me the most was seeing him put the same weight on his supposedly injured foot as he did the other.

I wasn't a doctor, but I was pretty sure he couldn't do that without experiencing some pain. Had he been pretending the whole time? And, if he had, why?

Tate, sensing my presence, jerked his head in my direction. His surprised expression quickly transformed to anger. "Who are you, and what are you doing back here?"

"I'm sorry," I muttered, taking a step back. "I was looking for the bathroom and must've taken a wrong turn." I was afraid he might recognize me since he'd seen me at the sandwich shop. Before he had a chance to say anything else, I scrambled to make a hasty exit. I couldn't stop thinking about what I'd seen or wonder why he'd need to fake an injury.

Maybe it was a ruse to attract female attention. He was a good-looking guy and had seemed personable when I'd overheard him flirting with Ivy. I found it hard to believe he'd need a prop to get a date. Since we'd never interacted, I didn't know enough about him or his personality that I could use for comparison.

I inhaled a deep breath before entering the reception area. Lou was nowhere in sight. If Adam and Zoey noticed my agitation, they didn't say anything.

"Did you have any other questions?" Adam asked.

I glanced at Zoey, who shook her head. "No, I think that'll do it," I said, taking a step toward the exit. I didn't think Tate would chase after me. But if I was wrong, I wanted to get out of there and avoid a possible scene with uncomfortable questions.

Adam slumped his shoulders, seemingly upset that we hadn't immediately asked to fill out membership contracts. He moved behind the counter and grabbed some brochures, handing one to each of us. "If you think of anything else, please don't hesitate to call. The number is on the back."

The guilt I felt knowing he'd never receive the call disappeared the instant I stepped outside and noticed Carson crossing the street at the corner. As soon as he spotted us, his even pace faltered for a brief moment. The odds of him showing up had been slim and made me wonder if the man had an internal radar capable of sensing my group's sleuthing agenda.

"This is not good," I muttered in a low voice so only Zoey could hear me.

"What are you talking about?" Zoey asked innocently, noting the direction of my gaze.

She must not have been around when Carson warned Delia, Myrna, Vincent, and me not to snoop in his cases. Either that, or she didn't believe he'd actually follow through on his threats. "Carson's going to figure out we were asking questions about Derek, and he won't be happy about it."

"Oh" was all she got out before Carson reached us.

I didn't have to see his eyes to know his sunglasses shielded one of his intense glares. "Ladies." Carson's expression was grim, and his tone lacked all qualities of a pleasant greeting. "Are you lost?"

It was an odd choice of words, but I recognized the underlying meaning. I hadn't prepared an excuse ahead of time and grasped for a reason Zoey and I were in the area of town that didn't involve our real reason for visiting the gym. Our attire wasn't helping the situation, but if there'd been stores nearby, coming up with something that involved shopping might have worked.

"As a matter of fact, we are…or were," Zoey said in an unbelievably calm and smooth voice.

I was glad she'd interceded on my behalf because my heart was pounding, and I was certain anything I said would come out a little raspier than normal.

"We were on our way to check out a tennis shoe sale for Myrna," Zoey said. "Some of the guys on our volleyball team were raving about Haskell's Gym, so we decided to check it out since we were in the neighborhood."

Zoey was good. I was certain in another life she'd make

an excellent spy. Unfortunately, Carson didn't seem convinced. "Uh-huh," he said, crossing his arms and causing his thick muscles to stretch the sleeves of his uniform top.

"You can check out my brochure if you're interested." I finally found my voice and held up the flyer Adam had given me.

"No, that's okay." Carson removed his sunglasses and slipped them into the pocket of his shirt. "Try to stay out of trouble." He stepped around us and entered the gym.

If he started asking questions, Adam and Lou could corroborate our story. If he talked to Jacob and asked about our visit, we'd be in trouble. "Come on," I said, grabbing Zoey's elbow, hoping to be long gone by the time that happened.

CHAPTER FOURTEEN

One of the great things about being a manager of a beachside coffee shop was having the flexibility to chat with customers. Now that the morning rush was over, I wanted to fill Myrna and Vincent in on what I'd learned from Jacob at the gym the day before. Delia was already caught up since we chatted during my evening walk with Harley.

Zoey stayed inside to take care of any new arrivals. Archer was also interested in hearing about our progress and had snagged a cup of coffee before leaning against the outside deck railing. Harley had settled into his usual spot near my aunt's feet and was napping when I stepped outside. After giving his head a scratch, I turned my chair to monitor the inside of the shop. If things got busy again, I didn't want Zoey to be stuck handling things on her own.

I sipped on my latte and listened while the gang provided Archer with details. I preferred flavored coffees but tried different drinks throughout the week, so I'd be familiar with everything we served in case customers asked for recommendations.

"So far, it sounds like the money angle is the only clue you have for Derek's death," Archer said.

"Yep," I said. "According to Brady, Derek crossed a lot of people on that front even before he moved here."

Archer speculatively rubbed his chin. "Finding out who was mad enough to murder him isn't going to be easy."

I'd reached the same conclusion and wasn't happy about it. "Did you know Derek?" I asked. Archer wasn't known to gossip, but he was still a good source of information. He'd lived in the area the longest and, because of his business, knew quite a few of the locals. Maybe he could provide some helpful insight about who else might qualify as a suspect.

"I knew of him but never met the man," Archer said. "I've known the Sharpe's since they opened their sandwich shop. Amelia mentioned Derek being the reason Ivy had moved here."

"And I'll bet she wasn't happy about it," I said. I'd already seen Amelia in action, so asking him what she'd said wasn't necessary.

Archer chuckled. "No, she wasn't."

"How did your visit to the gym go?" Myrna asked. If she was upset about being turned down for the trip, she wasn't showing it.

"Carson showed up as we were leaving," I said. "I don't think he was totally convinced that Zoey and I were at the gym to check out becoming members, but he didn't issue any warnings or toss us in jail." The latter was what I worried about the most because he threatened to do it enough times to make me believe he was serious.

"At least not yet," Myrna said, smirking.

Vincent groaned and rolled his eyes.

"Anyway, I talked to Jacob, and I think we can cross him off the list," I said. "He admitted he didn't like Derek because of his feelings for Natalie. I didn't sense that he hated him enough to kill him to get her back, though."

"Did you ask him about Derek's new business?" Delia asked.

"Uh-huh." I took another sip. "He didn't know

anything about it but said Derek might have shared the information with Natalie."

"She's never impressed me as being reliable, but it couldn't hurt to talk to her," Delia said.

It was good to know I wasn't the only one who had doubts about Natalie's truthfulness. "Okay. Does anyone know where she works?"

If we were close friends, we could show up at her home under the guise of offering our condolences. Since we weren't, I was afraid Natalie would get suspicious if we started asking a lot of personal questions about Derek.

"She works at Melanie's Clothes Closet, which happens to be her mother's clothes store," Delia said.

Showing up at a place of business was a lot less conspicuous. It would be easier to coerce Natalie into sharing information if she believed she'd be making sales. Which, of course, she would if I found something I wanted to purchase.

"If we time it right, we might be able to chat with Melanie as well," Delia added.

I didn't have to ask to glean what she was thinking. Some mothers and daughters shared secrets. Perhaps these two fell into that category, and we'd get lucky.

"Maybe we can get in a little shopping while we're there." Myrna wiggled her brows at Vincent. "Do you want to come along?"

Vincent groaned. "I don't need a new purse, but thanks for asking."

Myrna wasn't done teasing the men in our group. "Archer?"

Amusement flickered in his eyes. "I'm not in need of any new feminine items either."

Myrna was the first to giggle. It wasn't long before the rest of us joined in with a bout of laughter.

"Ladies, I'm up for a shopping trip this afternoon if you are," I said.

"Absolutely," Delia said.

"It's a date," Myrna said.

"Great." I noticed some new arrivals inside and pushed out of my seat. "I'll see you when I get off work."

CHAPTER FIFTEEN

I didn't like keeping things from Zoey, but given her desire to figuratively strangle Natalie for bad-mouthing Brady, asking her to go along on the trip to Melanie's place would've been counterproductive. I waited until I was on my way home to call the store and confirm that Natalie was working. I hated hanging up on the woman who'd assured me she was there, but I couldn't risk Natalie recognizing my voice.

Since Delia knew where we were going, she'd volunteered to drive, which was fine by me after an exhausting day at work. She'd also been nice enough to take Harley for a walk. All I had to do was change out of my work clothes when I got home.

We picked up Myrna along the way. The trip was relaxing, and I got to see a new part of town. The calm I'd enjoyed didn't last long. As excited as I was about checking out Melanie's shop, I wasn't looking forward to talking to Natalie. Dread settled in my stomach as soon as I got out of the car.

If Jacob was right about her having information pertaining to Derek's new business, then it was a necessary conversation if my friends and I wanted to prove Brady's innocence. I wasn't sure how much of what I'd learned would be the truth, so I'd have to pick through the details and confirm everything she told me.

Quite a few of the shop owners in town, the Bean included, used pastel or bold colors when painting the exterior of their buildings. Melanie was no different. She'd chosen a deep burgundy with a complementary pink trim around the front door and display windows. It was actually a good marketing technique because her place was more noticeable than the businesses on either side of her.

The interior walls were painted a light shade of mauve, and the trim was a similar pink to the one used on the outside of the building. The white shelves were stocked with an assortment of handbags and jewelry. The clothes racks contained a variety of fashions, everything from shorts to shirts to different styles of dresses.

The place wasn't overly busy, but there were a handful of women of varying ages perusing different parts of the store. I didn't see Melanie, but that didn't mean she wasn't around. Most retail places kept additional inventory in storerooms, so she could easily be working somewhere in the back.

"Try not to ruffle Natalie's feathers too much because I'm not leaving until I check out those sales over there," Myrna said, pointing to the other side of the room.

Seeing the signs posted in the center of several of the circular racks reminded me of when I was younger, and Delia and I would make a day of searching for the best bargains. "I'll do my best." I released a nervous giggle. Natalie seemed to like attention and had already demonstrated dramatic tendencies. I wasn't sure if my 'best' would be sufficient to keep her from overreacting.

"Here she comes, so you better get your shopping in now," Delia said.

"Sounds like a plan," Myrna said, then scurried toward the farthest rack.

I had to grin at my aunt's ingenuity. Myrna wasn't

known for being tactful. Sending her off to shop would make questioning Natalie, and possibly Melanie if she made an appearance, less confrontational.

Natalie approached us with a confident stride, her heels clicking on the floor's ceramic tiles. She was wearing a slimming yellow dress that reached the middle of her thighs and a white short-sleeve bodice jacket. She maintained a pleasant smile but narrowed her eyes. "Good afternoon, Delia." She shifted her gaze to me. "Brinley, right?"

"Yes," I said, smiling.

"What can I help you with today?"

"I need some new tops for work." Which happened to be the truth. Wearing an apron didn't prevent the occasional splash or spill of coffee from staining my clothes. Most of the spots came out, but only if I caught them in time. "We heard you were having a sale." I tipped my head toward the rack Myrna was rummaging through.

I glanced around to make sure we didn't have an audience. "We also wanted to make sure you were okay, you know, after what happened to your boyfriend."

"I appreciate that," Natalie said. "I'm doing okay, but I'll be even better once the police do their job." Her voice had gone up several notches, and I was afraid if I pushed her too hard, she'd start screeching.

"What makes you think they're not doing their job?" I asked, hoping a softened tone would placate her.

Natalie slapped her hands and her hips and huffed, "Because they haven't arrested Brady yet."

The young woman who'd been working behind the cash register when we arrived must've thought Natalie needed rescuing and headed in our direction. Thankfully, Delia noticed her too and moved to intercept her before she could reach us. Whatever my aunt said earned Natalie and me a forced smile from the woman before they headed to a display of blouses hanging on the far wall.

"Is there a reason you think he's responsible for

Derek's death?" I asked.

"Isn't it obvious?" Natalie asked.

I shrugged. "Not really." I had a hunch appearing ignorant would appeal to Natalie's ego and keep her talking. "I haven't lived in the area long enough to figure things out yet. I don't suppose you'd be willing to tell me what you know, would you?"

Natalie rolled her eyes. When she took a step closer after shooting sidelong looks around the room, I could tell she was hooked. "Derek told me Brady was out to get him because he always had a thing for Ivy."

"But they were divorced, so what reason could he possibly have to kill your boyfriend?" I asked because her logic made no sense.

Natalie furrowed her brows as if contemplating what I'd said for the first time. "I...I hadn't thought of that. But now that you mention it, Ivy did seem surprised to see Derek when we stopped by her trailer the day of the volleyball game."

"Maybe it had something to do with his new business," I said. "Or a new partner." I didn't know if Derek had collaborated with someone else and added the last part on a whim.

"Do you think Tate had something to do with this?" Natalie asked.

"Tate?" I asked for clarification. I didn't think it was a coincidence that another man with the same name hung out with other people she knew.

"Yeah." Natalie bobbed her head. "They were both signed up for the volleyball tournament. Tate couldn't play, but you might have seen him at the game. He was hard to miss because he was wearing an ankle boot and using crutches."

"Oh, okay." Given Natalie's penchant for sharing exaggerated tidbits with the locals, I didn't tell her that Jackson had replaced Tate on one of the teams or that I knew he was friends with Ivy's brother James. And, most importantly, that he was faking his injury.

I was fairly sure if Natalie knew anything about Tate's charade, she'd be happy to share it with everyone. "Did Derek tell you what type of new business he planned to open?" I asked.

Natalie frowned. "No, and you'd think he would've at least shared the information with me since I was his girlfriend."

"Did he say why he didn't want you to know?" I asked, even though I was pretty sure it was because she couldn't keep a secret.

"He was afraid if certain people in town found out, it might cause problems." Natalie flipped her hair over her shoulder. "Now that I think about it, Tate used to complain to Derek about Lou Haskell's place all the time. Maybe they were planning to open another gym."

"Hmm," I said, agreeing. I had to give Natalie credit. Her suggestion was actually a reasonable deduction and worth checking out.

"Do you happen to know how Derek ended up with a black eye?" I asked. It was a minor detail, but there was always a chance it would provide a major clue. "Did he get into a fight with someone?"

"It's not what you think." Natalie waved her hand back and forth. "It was an accident. Derek got elbowed in the face during volleyball practice."

"Did you believe him?" I asked.

"Yes, because I was there when it happened." Natalie's gaze was drawn to a woman heading for the checkout counter. "I should get back to work."

"If you don't mind, I have one more question," I said, then asked, "Did Derek leave with you after the games?" He was still wearing his team outfit when he was murdered, which meant he hadn't gone home to change.

"No, he told me he had some business to take care of and stayed behind." Natalie blinked back the moisture building in her eyes. "Maybe if he'd gone with me, he'd still be alive."

I watched her hurry away, doubting there was anything she could have done to prevent Derek's death.

CHAPTER SIXTEEN

By the time Myrna, Delia, and I finished shopping at Melanie's place, it was late in the afternoon, and the temperature had dropped to a tolerable level, which made taking Harley for a walk in the park a pleasant experience. As soon as we reached my aunt's car, Myrna placed a call to Vincent, asking him to meet us so we could discuss what I'd learned from Natalie and figure out a way to proceed.

I kept Harley on his leash and paced in the grass across from Myrna, Delia, and Vincent, who'd taken a seat on the brick wall surrounding the fountain. There were other people out taking a stroll or walking their pets, but not too many that we had to worry about being overheard.

"What did Natalie have to say?" Vincent asked.

Before I could answer, the cell stashed in my hip pack alerted me to an incoming text. "Hold that thought," I said, slipping the loop of Harley's leash over my wrist so I could retrieve my phone. Seeing Jackson's name on the screen made me grin. Reading his message sent flutters to my stomach. *I'm looking forward to Saturday and checking in to make sure you haven't changed your mind.*

I hurried to type a response. *There's no way I'd pass on an opportunity to have ice cream.*

Only ice cream? He included a sad-faced emoji.

I giggled. *Maybe seeing you as well.*

Okay, then. My ego is doing much better. See you soon. His message included more emojis; one of an ice cream cone, the other a happy face.

I looked up to find Delia, Myrna, and Vincent staring at me and grinning.

"Care to share details with the group?" Myrna asked, though judging by her smirk, I was certain she already knew about my date with Jackson.

"Nooo, but I will share what I learned from Natalie." I tucked the phone away. "First of all, she confirmed the bruise near Derek's eye wasn't caused by a fight," I said. "He was accidentally elbowed in the face during practice."

"Well darn," Myrna groaned. "I was sure hoping that would turn out to be a good clue and lead us to the killer."

"I did too, but—"

"Hey, everyone," Ellie called, picking up her pace as she approached us. I'd noticed her walking Bruno on the other side of the park, but wasn't sure she'd seen us. She was dressed in light tan capri pants and sandals.

"Hi, Ellie," I said, amused because once she got closer and spotted Harley, she picked up her dog and cuddled him to her chest. Her worries were unfounded. I'd seen Harley playfully chase after Quincy enough times to know that he'd never hurt another animal. "How's it going?"

Ellie narrowed her eyes, then turned her head in both directions as if she expected someone to jump out from behind a palm tree. Satisfied that she was safe, she said, "Rumor has it our sweet Brady is a suspect in the recent murder."

"We heard the same thing," I said.

"Are you doing your sleuthing thing to prove he's innocent?" Ellie asked.

She glanced around again. "Because if you are, I think you should check out James Sharpe."

"Why do you think we should take a look at him?" Delia asked.

Ellie straightened her shoulders and stuck out her chin. "Because he was acting suspicious the other day at the game."

"Suspicious how?" I asked.

"I saw him following Brady."

I shared a curious look with the rest of the group. Ellie was fairly perceptive, but it was possible what she'd seen was the two men heading in the same direction. "How do you know?"

She gave me an exasperated look. "Because the few times Brady stopped, James ducked behind people to keep from being noticed."

Had Ellie seen James do something more than shadow Brady? Had he dug around in a trashcan and pulled out the to-go cup I'd spotted near Derek's body?

"Did James do anything else?" Myrna asked in a conspiratorial tone. She'd obviously figured out where I was going with my questions.

"I stopped watching him after that because I ran into Clara Jessop, and you know how she loves to talk." Ellie tsked. "Anyway, I got distracted, and by the time I headed back to my seat so I wouldn't miss the game, James was gone."

"Did you tell Carson what you saw?" I asked.

"No," Ellie huffed.

"Would you mind telling us why not?" I asked.

"Because he didn't bother to question me." Ellie seemed upset that she'd been overlooked.

I didn't want to hurt her feelings by pointing out that she hadn't been at the crime scene and the police had no reason to talk to her about Derek's murder.

"Besides, he'll think I'm an old lady who likes to make things up," Ellie said.

"Carson's usually reasonable." At least most of the time. "I think he'll want to hear what you have to say."

Though he'd be more inclined to believe her story if she'd seen James digging through the trash.

Ellie narrowed her eyes, still skeptical. "Do you really think so?"

"I do," I said, trying not to sound too convincing.

"I'll think about it." Ellie shifted sideways. "Right now, I need to get Bruno home and fix dinner."

I watched her leave and set her dog on the ground when she was halfway across the park and away from other animals.

Delia and Myrna knew Ellie better than I did. "Do you think she'll talk to Carson?"

"Probably not," Myrna said. "She's pretty set in her ways. If he doesn't visit her place or accidentally run into her somewhere, I don't think Carson will hear about it from her."

"Even if he did find out, Ellie could be right. He might discard the information as nonsense," Delia said.

"Ellie wouldn't make something like that up," Myrna said.

"I don't think she would either, which is why we shouldn't dismiss James as a suspect," Delia said.

"I agree." I took a few steps to the right to give Harley some leeway with his leash. "Maybe Derek's death had to do with money but not entirely for the reason we'd assumed."

Vincent crossed his arms and stretched out his legs. "Care to explain?"

"It's obvious James cares a great deal about his sister," I said. "He also didn't like Derek."

"Or Brady, for that matter," Delia added.

"I also think we should add Tate Levine to our list," I said.

"The name doesn't sound familiar," Vincent said. "Is there a reason we should know him?"

Vincent remembered everything. I must not have told him and Myrna how Jackson had replaced Tate on the volleyball team or why so I quickly filled them in.

"He's also a friend of James and Ivy Sharpe," Delia said.

"And, if the information I got from Natalie is reliable, he's also connected to Derek," I said.

"It sounds like you found out something important," Delia said.

"I did." I bobbed my head. "When we got together last, I forgot to mention I saw Tate in the shower area at the gym." I didn't want to be responsible for spreading rumors and hadn't told Zoey about the encounter either. After my conversation with Natalie, the details surrounding Tate's non-injury now seemed important.

"Oooh." Myrna wiggled her brows. "Was he naked?"

Vincent shot a sidelong glare at Myrna. "How is that relevant?"

Myrna shrugged and smirked. "I thought it was obvious."

I didn't give her a chance to share her views on the subject. "He was wearing a towel, and I didn't stick around long enough to gawk. I did, however, notice that he'd taken off his medical boot and was putting equal weight on both feet."

"That does seem interesting," Delia said. "I wonder what he's up to."

"At first, I thought it might be an insecurity issue when it came to women, but after Natalie told me Tate was Derek's new business partner, I'm not so sure," I said.

"Did she know anything about their business plans?" Vincent asked.

"Derek wouldn't tell her, but she did say Tate complained about Lou's place all the time and thought maybe they planned to open another gym," I said.

If I hadn't seen Tate without his boot, I might have considered Lou a suspect. If the older man wanted to get rid of the competition, he would've gotten rid of Tate as well. Someone had gone to a lot of trouble to leave Brady's to-go cup near the body, which made me believe the death was personal.

"Ellie made a good case for James being involved, but I don't think we should rule out Tate," I said.

"We can't establish alibis or get one of them to admit to their crime unless we talk to them," Vincent said. "Now that Brinley knows Tate's secret, he'll be guarded about talking to anyone."

"Maybe we should tell Carson what we've learned so far," Delia said.

If only it were that simple. The deputy was thorough and, no doubt, had questioned all the volleyball players, specifically those who played on Derek's team. He might have even spoken with Tate but would've dismissed him after seeing him on crutches. It was my word against Tate's, and I had no way of proving he wasn't injured. "He'll tell us it's circumstantial, then lecture us for interfering," I said.

"Or follow through on his threat to put us in jail," Myrna said.

Yeah, there was definitely a risk of that. "What we need is some real evidence," I said.

"Or a confession," Vincent said.

I agreed but wasn't sure how we were going to go about getting either one of those things. I thought about his comment regarding Tate, and a plan began to form in my mind. "I might have an idea, but it's a little risky."

Myrna rubbed her hands together. "Will it be life-threatening or involve the use of weapons?"

"Seriously?" Delia asked.

Myrna shrugged. "It's a legitimate question."

I suppressed a giggle. "We won't need any weapons, but things could get a little dangerous." I was going to be the bait in my scenario. If everything played out the way I imagined it in my head, then I'd be the only one who'd be putting myself in harm's way. Since I wasn't a fan of getting hurt, I planned to utilize every precaution possible.

"Before Brinley shares any details, I think we should head back to my place and order some pizza," Delia said, pushing to her feet.

"I like that plan," I said, smiling.

"Me too," Myrna said. "The walk will give me time to come up with some good reasons why being armed is a good thing."

"Myrna," Vincent and Delia growled at the same time.

"What?" she asked as she slid off the wall. "Private investigators are allowed to be armed, aren't they?"

"Yes, but we're nothing more than amateur sleuths," Vincent said.

Myrna harrumphed. "Speak for yourself."

I shook my head and tugged on Harley's leash. The next few hours were definitely going to be a challenge and most likely entertaining.

CHAPTER SEVENTEEN

Delia, Myrna, Vincent, and I were venturing into an area of sleuthing I would've strongly opposed several months ago. Normally, our investigations remained within the parameters of questioning suspects and gathering clues. Brady was a friend, his sister Avery even more so. Whoever had taken Derek's life had crossed a line when they decided to frame him for the crime, and I was determined to discover the culprit's identity.

After reviewing all the information we'd obtained, we unanimously agreed that James, Tate, or maybe both were the most likely candidates for the murder.

Though we hadn't uncovered a reason, the fact they'd both kept Derek's relocation to town from Ivy bothered me. Then there was Ellie's visual confirmation that James had followed Brady during the tournament. Which occurred not long after Delia and I'd overheard him voice his dislike for Brady to his sister. What Ellie had told us was only hearsay, but she had no reason to make something like that up.

Since we couldn't narrow it down to one or the other, we decided to start with Tate. If it turned out he wasn't responsible for Derek's death, we'd move on to James.

Determining a location and coming up with a way to get Tate to meet me posed the biggest problem. The area had to be fairly isolated yet also provide places for my aunt and friends to hide if I ran into trouble.

The police hadn't released the crime scene yet. The Sharpe's trailer, along with the other vendor booths, were still in place. Pedestrian traffic would be low late in the day, so we decided it was an ideal spot for a meeting, not to mention ironic if we'd deduced the killer's identity correctly.

Thanks to Vincent and his connections, which he refused to reveal, finding Tate's cell number had been easier than I thought. Vincent was worried our suspect might have some kind of caller ID on his phone and suggested we find an alternative for making the call. I had to remind him that Tate had already seen my face and had to assume I knew his foot injury wasn't real. With a little effort, it wouldn't be hard for him to track me down if he thought I was a threat, which included where I lived and worked.

Besides, if everything turned out the way it was supposed to, then the killer would end up in jail, and knowing my identity wouldn't be a concern. Of course, there was always the possibility we'd missed an important clue and were headed in the wrong direction.

If I wasn't right about Tate, then I'd apologize for the misunderstanding and promise to keep his secret. The same would go for James, less the secret part. Though, if he was innocent, I doubted after being accused of a terrible crime, he'd be happy to see me in his shop. Which was too bad because the Sharpe's made some of the best cookies I'd ever tasted.

We'd also revisited the topic of whether or not we should tell someone in law enforcement what we'd discovered so far. We weren't equipped to handle things if something went wrong and the situation turned ugly or life-threatening.

None of us was comfortable going to Carson, which was how we ended up with Douglas standing in the middle of Delia's living room, glaring at us. I'd caught him off-duty and out of uniform. He was dressed in shorts and a T-shirt.

"You did what?" Douglas asked, pinching the bridge of his nose.

For the second time in a matter of minutes, I explained how I'd sent a text to Tate earlier in the day that read: *I know your secret and what you did. I haven't told anyone yet, so we need to talk about a beneficial arrangement.* I also added a time and place where we should meet.

Tate hadn't responded to my text, but I'd adjusted the settings on my phone with a read receipt and knew he'd received the message. What I didn't know was whether or not he'd make an appearance. If he was guilty, I was certain he wouldn't pass on an opportunity to talk. If he was innocent, he'd either ignore my request or show up to satisfy his curiosity.

"I still can't believe you did that. Don't you know trying to blackmail a potential killer is dangerous?" Douglas growled. "I should haul all of you down to the station right now." His irritated gaze jumped from Vincent to Delia to Myrna, then ended with me.

Douglas harbored a secret crush on Zoey and would no doubt help us to impress her. I didn't want to influence the direction of a possible relationship between them, which was why I'd left her out of our plans on purpose. I'd risked her being angry for being omitted but decided to worry about it later.

"I think you've been hanging out with Carson way too much because you're starting to sound a lot like him," Myrna said in a non-complimentary tone.

"I don't care," Douglas said. "Do you have any idea how angry he's going to be when he finds out?"

I did know. "That's why we called you instead." Douglas was also relatively new to law enforcement. I could understand his trepidation and hoped to alleviate some of his concern by adding, "If we're wrong, Tate won't show, and you can continue investigating. But if we're right, and you catch the killer, you'll be a hero."

"Yeah," Douglas groaned sarcastically. "I don't think my boss is going to see it that way. And neither will the sheriff."

Delia cringed, reminding me how much she despised Landon Lennox. He'd asked her out on a date long before I'd arrived in town and hadn't taken her refusal well. His grudge had included having Carson treat her as a suspect because she'd had lunch with Myles Mumford prior to his murder.

Before I could come up with a rational way to make him feel better, Douglas retrieved his cell from his pocket. "You know I have to call this in, right?"

Myrna snatched the phone from his hand. "Not until after we apprehend the killer." She hopped around like a bunny, and I worried she might fall and hurt herself.

Luckily, my aunt had more experience when it came to dealing with Myrna and grabbed the phone away from her. "We are officially cutting you off from watching detective shows."

Myrna stopped bouncing and shot an I-dare-you-to-try glare at my aunt.

"If he wants to let a killer get away, we can't stop him." Delia handed the phone back to Douglas. My aunt might not have any children of her own, but she knew how to act like a parent. Age didn't matter, nor did the level of guilt someone experienced when she used her disappointed look.

I could tell by Douglas's wavering expression that he was carefully weighing his options.

"What's it going to be?" Myrna shot him a scary narrow-eyed glare. "Help us solve a crime or kiss the boss's backside?"

Technically, he could arrest us for interfering in police

business, so I didn't think Myrna giving him an ultimatum was a wise decision.

I knew she'd won Douglas over when he clamped his lips and amusement flickered in his eyes. "Okay, okay. You win." He waved his hands in front of him. "Just so you know, you two are worse than my mother."

Douglas was a great guy with a big heart. Mrs. Dankworth had done a good job raising her son, but I wasn't sure if she would've thought much of the comparison. "We appreciate the help."

"Don't thank me yet," Douglas said. "If things go badly, you're dealing with Carson on your own."

I chuckled. "Fair enough."

"Knowing you guys, I'm guessing there's more to your plan than a covert rendezvous," he said.

"There is," I said, grinning. "We'll explain on the way." I headed for the kitchen. "Let me take care of Harley first."

Even after receiving a doggy treat and being told I wouldn't be gone long, my dog wasn't happy to be left behind. I could hear him whining after I closed the door to join the others who were waiting near Delia's car. I didn't know what to expect once we arrived at our destination, and wasn't willing to risk my furry companion getting hurt.

We got to the beach a good half hour before my scheduled meet with Tate and parked the vehicle a block away.

"Don't let him get too close," Douglas said once we'd all exited the vehicle. "And don't be afraid to scream for help if you feel threatened."

"I won't," I said, shuddering. The memory I had of the stake sticking out of Derek's chest was all the incentive I needed to heed his words.

I waited for everyone to find a place to hide, which equated to them ducking down beside the car before I headed for my destination alone.

The sun was slowly making its descent on the horizon.

Even though there was plenty of light, and it wouldn't be completely dark for a while yet, I couldn't stop the feeling of dread surging through my system. The ocean's slowly rippling waves, which often had a calming effect, did nothing to help my building anxiety.

I hadn't ventured to this area of the beach since the day Ivy found Derek's body. Other than the string of flags, which were drooping in places, everything looked pretty much the same.

Vincent had his binoculars with him, so as long as I remained in the open, I wasn't worried about being seen.

Time progressed slowly, and my lack of patience had me pacing the sidewalk. Other than a random seagull and a man out jogging, who smiled and nodded as he ran past me, the area was deserted.

I checked the clock on my phone, noting that it was fifteen minutes after the time I'd included in my text. I still hadn't received a response or gotten a visual of Tate and figured our efforts had been wasted. I was about to head back to the group when I noticed movement on the other side of the dead-end street.

Tate, dressed in a tank top, shorts, and tennis shoes, strolled in my direction. It seemed that after being caught at the gym, he didn't think it was necessary to continue faking his injury.

In case he had a weapon stuffed in his pocket, I wanted to maintain some distance and took a step back when he got closer.

He stopped and held up his hands in a placating manner. "You're the one who sent the text, right?"

"Yes."

"So you know my name, but I don't know yours." Curiosity was the only thing I detected in Tate's voice, not the threatening tone I'd expected.

"It's Brinley," I said.

"Well, Brinley, I get that you uncovered my secret." He swept his hand toward his feet. "But I have no idea what awful thing you think I did or why it requires some kind of an arrangement."

If I wanted a confession, I couldn't start by accusing him of murder. I needed to ask him questions and hope he filled in the gaps on his own. "We'll get to that in a minute, but first, I'd like to know why the pretense with your foot."

"I really did sprain my foot the day before the volleyball tournament," Tate said. "The medical boot and crutches were from an injury I'd gotten a few years ago." His cheeks reddened, and he stared at the ground. "I used them because I knew I'd get extra attention from the ladies."

Jackson had pegged that one correctly. "I heard you and Derek were going into business together," I said. "Did you have a falling out?"

"No." He frowned and signed. "Let me guess. You talked to Natalie," Tate said. "You can't always rely on what she says. Most of the time, she tends to get things wrong or exaggerates the details of what she hears. Derek did approach me about being his partner, but I turned him down."

He apparently knew Natalie better than I did, so I had no reason to doubt him.

"Wait," Tate said, widening his eyes. "Do you think I killed Derek? Is that why you wanted to meet me here?"

I quirked a brow and crossed my arms but remained silent. Now that he was talking freely, I didn't want to interrupt.

Tate nervously glanced behind me at the police tape marking off the spot where Derek's body had been found. "I swear I didn't have anything to do with his murder." He ran his hands along the side of his head. "You have to believe me. The only thing I'm guilty of is poor judgment."

His panic seemed authentic, and I found myself empathizing with him. I wasn't perfect when it came to judging someone's character, but I no longer thought Tate was the killer.

"Word of advice," I said. "Women like guys who don't pretend to be something they're not."

CHAPTER EIGHTEEN

Douglas didn't stick around long after we left the beach and returned to Delia's house. I shared the details of my interaction with Tate during the drive. Douglas wouldn't admit it, but I got the impression he was also hoping we'd discovered the identity of the killer.

This wasn't the first time Vincent, Myrna, Delia, and I had missed something important and got things wrong. It didn't happen very often and had always been while we were playing our online mystery game.

The real-life experience was majorly disheartening. "I'm sorry, guys," I said, glancing around Delia's living room and taking in the disappointed faces. "I was sure we were close, that either Tate or James murdered Derek." Based on the clues I'd uncovered, I had more reason to believe Tate was the killer. I hadn't gleaned anything new from our conversation and was convinced he wasn't our guy. We had even less to go on for James, so reaching out to him might be moot.

I knew in my heart that Brady was innocent. The only thing that would make me feel worse was having to face Avery if her brother got arrested for the crime.

Delia put her hand on my shoulder. "You have nothing

to apologize for. We all came to the same conclusion."

"She's right," Myrna said, plopping down on the couch next to Luna, then pulling the cat onto her lap before she could escape. Luna had a snooty attitude and might act like she didn't want any attention, but her loud purrs suggested otherwise. "I say we order some pizza and figure out a new plan of attack."

"That works for me," Vincent said, retrieving his cell phone and tapping in a number.

My aunt kept to-go menus from a lot of the local food places in a drawer in the kitchen, but we rarely had to use them. We'd ordered from the pizzeria plenty of times, so Vincent knew what we wanted without asking.

Their optimism was infectious and had me grinning. "While we're waiting, I'm going to take Harley for a walk."

"Would you like some company?" Delia asked.

"No, I'm good." I hooked the leash to my dog's collar. "We shouldn't be gone long." I slid open the screen door leading to the deck and beach at the back of the house.

The sun was slowly disappearing from the sky. Pinks and yellows with a smidge of purple colored the horizon. I hadn't planned to go far, but it would be dark soon. I wanted to ensure I could see where I was going, and flipped the switch for the outside lighting.

"Harley," I said, bending over to scratch his head once we'd reached the sand. "I'm missing something important, but I have no idea what it is. How about you, any clue?"

I hadn't expected a response and was surprised when he barked. He tugged on his leash, his attention drawn to something moving in the shadows two houses over.

"It's okay, boy," I cooed when a person stepped out where I could see them. They were dressed in black from top to bottom, but I could tell from their silhouette that it was a woman. The temperature was starting to drop, but the air was still warm. The hooded sweatshirt concealing her face seemed a bit much.

Harley calmed but only a little. He stayed near my leg,

prancing nervously. When the woman pulled back her hood, I squinted to make sure I was seeing correctly. "Melanie?" She didn't live in Delia's neighborhood or in the nearby retirement community, so I couldn't think of a reason for her to be roaming this area of the beach. "What are you doing here?"

"I came to talk." The strain in her voice set off my internal warning system, alerting me that something wasn't right.

My dog hadn't taken care of business, but I was certain it wasn't safe to remain outside. "Sure," I said, taking a step toward the house. "Why don't we go inside?"

"No." Melanie gritted out as she moved to block my path.

I glanced at the lighted windows behind her, hoping to catch someone's attention. Unfortunately, I didn't see anyone. Melanie looked poised to attack, so pushing the issue didn't seem like a good idea. Delia would eventually come looking for me, but not until after the pizza arrived. Keeping Melanie busy until then was the best I could do. "Okay. What did you want to talk about?"

"You need to stop asking people questions about Derek's murder."

Because of her business and connection with a non-profit organization, Melanie knew quite a few people in town. She could've found out from any number of sources. "Who—"

"Natalie told me," Melanie said, cutting me off.

I wasn't sure why her daughter had singled me out. Delia and Myrna had gone to the store with me. Maybe Natalie had only mentioned me because I was the one who'd talked to her the longest.

Melanie's eyes were wide, and the light coming from the back of Delia's house hit the side of her face, giving her an ominous look. "My daughter isn't necessarily naive, but she is headstrong. She refused to listen to anything I had to say about that despicable man. After I learned what he'd done to Ivy, I wasn't about to let him do the same thing to Natalie."

"I assume you're talking about Derek," I said.

"Yes," she hissed. "He got what he deserved, and you need to leave it alone...or else."

"Or else what?" I was almost afraid to ask, but I had a feeling I was staring at Derek's killer and wanted clarification.

"This." Melanie shoved her hand in her jacket pocket and pulled out a switchblade, which she immediately flicked open, the clicking noise making me jump. Harley sensed the impending danger and released a low growl as he moved closer to me.

I wanted to reach down and reassure my dog that everything would be okay but was afraid if I broke eye contact with Melanie, she might attack.

"Brinley. Are you out here?" I couldn't remember ever being so happy to hear Carson's voice or see him step out onto my aunt's deck. I wondered if Douglas was the reason the deputy had made an appearance. The moment didn't last long because Melanie growled, then turned and started running.

I didn't think Carson had heard her confession, and I didn't know if he'd seen her face. I wasn't inclined to mess with someone wielding a knife, but if she escaped now, it would be her word against mine. I wasn't about to let her get away with Derek's murder.

"Here!" I yelled. "Melanie just confessed to killing Derek." I dropped Harley's leash and took off after her. I'd never played football, never tackled anyone to the ground, and never been mistaken for a ninja. With adrenaline pumping through my system, I launched myself at Melanie's back and forced her face-first into the sand.

Luckily, she'd dropped the knife, so I didn't have to worry about getting cut or stabbed.

"Get off me," she screamed and bucked, trying to dislodge me.

Harley had trailed after me and was pacing in the sand near Melanie's head and barking. I wasn't sure I'd be able to hold her much longer. Fortunately, Carson arrived and tapped my shoulder. "I can take it from here." He moved in quickly after I rolled away from Melanie, then tugged her to her feet and slapped his handcuffs to her wrists.

"Are you okay?" Carson asked, offering me a hand up.

"I'm fine," I said, smiling. "Thanks for the rescue." I expected him to point out that I wouldn't need his help if my friends and I hadn't been sniffing around his case. Instead, he tipped his head and said, "No problem. I'm getting used to it."

"Melanie dropped her knife over there somewhere," I said, wiggling my finger at the ground a few feet away. I didn't think the weapon had been used to kill anyone. At least I hoped not, but still wasn't going to pick it up without Carson's approval.

Delia, Myrna, and Vincent arrived as he closed the blade and stuck it in his pocket. Myrna hastened to pick up Harley and cuddle him to her chest.

"Are you hurt?" Delia asked, her voice frantic as she ran her hands along my arms.

"I'm all right, thanks to Carson." I wasn't sure that would've been my answer if he hadn't shown up when he had. I held out my shaking hands, and Harley gladly jumped in my arms, then proceeded to lick my face. Clutching him to my chest and receiving doggy kisses was better than taking medicine to calm my jittery nerves.

Delia gave Carson an appreciative smile. "What prompted your visit?"

"Douglas told me about your stunt with Tate, so I thought I'd stop by and have a chat before heading home," Carson said.

So much for not getting a lecture.

Carson placed a call to the station and requested backup. Melanie didn't appear happy about being cuffed but didn't struggle when he wrapped a hand around her arm and led her to the deck with the rest of us following.

"Have a seat," he said after pulling out a chair from the patio table and urging her to sit. "While we're waiting, why don't you tell me what happened." He directed the question to me.

I spent the next few minutes giving him the details of my conversation with Melanie. When I finished, he turned to Melanie. "Is there anything you want to add?"

"Only that this was Derek's fault," Melanie said. "If he'd stayed in Clarksburry where he belonged, he'd still be alive."

"You can't go around ending someone's life just because you don't like their relocation choices," Myrna said.

"You don't understand," Melanie snarled. "He was going to ruin Natalie's life the same way he did Ivy's. Can you imagine the damage it would cause my reputation if that happened?"

Now we were getting to the heart of the matter. It wasn't only her daughter she was concerned about; it was herself.

"Too bad you're plan didn't work," Myrna said. "All you did was manage to ruin both of your reputations."

The ramifications of what Melanie had done finally registered. She opened her mouth as if she wanted to refute Myrna's claim, then closed it without saying anything.

It wouldn't be long before a police officer came to get Melanie. I had a few unanswered questions and figured this was the best time to ask them. "How did you get Derek to meet with you?"

Melanie sneered. "That was easy. I told him I'd heard he was starting a new business, and I had a proposition I wanted to discuss with him. His greed got the better of him. He didn't even balk when I suggested we meet on the beach after everyone left."

"What I don't understand is why you made it look as if

Brady was the one who killed Derek," I said.

Carson raised a brow. He'd obviously been curious about the same thing because he didn't put a stop to my questions.

"At first, I didn't care who got blamed as long as it wasn't me," Melanie said. "I knew Brady and Derek had been friends once. I got the idea to frame him after I saw him toss his to-go cup from Sharpe's in the trash."

"Did you know that Brady moved here to get away from Derek?" I asked, unable to keep the disdain from my voice. "He wanted to improve his life the same as Ivy. And you nearly ruined it for him."

"It sounds like you're no better than Derek," Delia said.

"So it looks like you're both getting what you deserve," Myrna said.

I wasn't one for gloating, but I couldn't help smiling at the irony in her words.

CHAPTER NINETEEN

With Melanie confessing to the murder and going to jail, Carson had no reason to leave the crime scene taped off on the beach. Given the circumstances surrounding Derek's death, the remainder of the volleyball tournament had been canceled. Having one of their members be responsible for taking a life had caused a lot of publicity, and not the good kind. The committee announced that this year's tournament was a tie and provided each team with their own trophy.

Avery had stopped by my aunt's house to personally thank us for clearing her brother and drop off a box containing one of Tori's cheesecakes. Payment hadn't been necessary, but none of us was willing to refuse her gift.

I was glad when the day of my date with Jackson finally arrived. Because I'd been anxious and looking forward to our time together, the hours seemed to go by slowly. Work had been busy. Melanie being apprehended by the police was the main topic circulating throughout the Bean. The locals who weren't regular customers stopped by to share in the spreading gossip. Even the visiting tourists showed an interest in hearing what everyone had to say.

At one point, after being exhausted from answering the

same questions too many times, Archer stepped in and told me to take a break outside with Delia, Myrna, and Vincent. During the morning rush, they'd also been bombarded with questions, but not nearly as much as me.

The early evening weather was warm and humid. Jackson and I had decided to spend the majority of our date outside. I wanted to look nice, but I didn't want to wear anything that would make me uncomfortable. I'd gone with a stylish tank top and belted skirt that reached mid-thigh. I'd also selected a pair of sandals that could easily be slipped off if we decided to go for a walk on the beach. Since I wore my hair back in ponytails for work, I let my tawny strands flow freely over my shoulders.

Jackson had shown up at my aunt's house wearing a button-down shirt with short sleeves, a pair of casual-style shorts, and light tan deck shoes. Our outing was a double date of sorts since we'd agreed to bring along our pets.

When Jackson had first told me he had a dog, I'd imagined Rocky to be a larger breed, like a Labrador or a collie, maybe even a German Shepard. I hadn't expected an adorable Jack Russell Terrier. Other than terrorizing Luna, introducing Harley and Rocky had gone well.

Frigid Fantasy Flavors had a drive-through, making it easy to place our order without having to worry about leaving our pets unsupervised in Jackson's car. When he caught me eying the amount on his gift certificate, he told me to get whatever I wanted and not to worry about the cost.

We ended up parking in the lot near the Bean. After unleashing the dogs so they could run on the beach, we settled at a table on the shop's deck. The place was closed, and I knew if Archer happened by, he wouldn't mind us hanging out.

"This was a great idea," I said, watching Harley and Rocky chase each other across the sand. Their antics were playful and had me giggling.

Jackson had been genuinely concerned when I told him

about my confrontation with Melanie. I appreciated that he hadn't gone into an overprotective mode or tried to persuade me not to do any future sleuthing, like a certain deputy I knew.

"So essentially, Melanie got rid of Derek because she didn't want him dating her daughter, stealing her money, and potentially ruining her life," Jackson said, then scooped a spoonful of his cotton candy ice cream from his sundae container. He wasn't afraid to admit he loved sprinkles, something I found endearing, and had requested extra when placing his order.

When it came to the delicious treat, I had two favorites: mint chip and chocolate fudge ripple. After the week I'd had, I treated myself to the ripple coated with an extra layer of hot fudge.

"Basically, yes." I licked the excess fudge stuck to my spoon. "She was also worried about the damage Natalie's relationship with Derek would cause her own reputation." Which I thought was selfish. "I don't think Melanie considered how the one thing she was trying to avoid would happen to Natalie if she got caught."

"From what you've told me, it sounds like Melanie was convinced no one would find out it was her," Jackson said.

"That's true, and it might be why Melanie showed up early the day after the murder. She'd probably wanted to monitor the crime's progress and see if Brady got blamed for her framing efforts."

"Are you talking about Brady Noonan, the landscape maintenance guy?"

"Yeah, do you know him?" I asked.

Jackson nodded. "He does my grandfather's yard. He seems like a nice guy, so why would Melanie want to frame him?"

I spent the next few minutes explaining what I knew of their history and the dynamics between Brady, Ivy, and Derek. "Melanie said Brady was her initial target, but I think she would've been okay if Ivy got blamed. I think that's why she picked the area near the Sharpe's trailer as her meeting spot with Derek."

"Wow," Jackson said, winking. "You've given this some thought. I'm impressed."

I stuck some ice cream in my mouth, hoping the cold would counteract the heat scorching my face. "Myrna, Vincent, and Delia helped." I was unwilling to take all the credit. "I think Melanie only came after me because she didn't know Delia and Myrna had been in the store with me when I'd talked to Natalie." A fact I was grateful for because the crazed woman might have gone after them as well.

Jackson placed his spoon in his empty container and pushed it aside. "I'm glad everything turned out okay and you didn't get hurt." He paused for a moment, then slipped his hand behind my neck and pressed his lips to mine. It was our first kiss, and I eagerly melted into it.

"Mmm," he said, pulling back and licking his lower lip. "Have I mentioned how much I like chocolate?"

I laughed. "I thought you were a cotton candy kind of guy."

He grinned, forming irresistible dimples. "I have no problem diversifying."

"Good to know."

"Or doing additional testing before making a decision." When Jackson leaned in for another kiss, I spotted Quincy emerging from behind a palm tree and knew what would happen next. "Oh, no," I muttered.

"What?" Jackson straightened in his seat, his gaze alert as he searched the beach for impending danger.

"How does Rocky feel about cats? He doesn't like to eat them, does he?" The instant the dogs noticed Quincy, I was on my feet and heading toward the stairs.

"I don't think so," Jackson said, trailing after me. "Why?"

"Because we're about to find out."

"Harley, Rocky, no!" I yelled, hurrying to catch up with

them. I could've saved my breath. As soon as Quincy disappeared between the trees, both dogs stopped, displaying an air of triumph as they padded toward me.

"Was that Quincy?" Jackson asked.

I'd told him about my efforts to bond with the cat. "Yes, but I'm afraid the boys may have set my relationship building back a bit."

"I have no doubt your determination will win in the end."

"Thanks. I hope so," I said, making sure Quincy hadn't returned before facing Jackson.

"Is hanging out with you always going to be this exciting?"

If he hadn't slipped his arms around my waist, his question would've made me nervous. Instead, my pulsed race. "Why? Are you having second thoughts about being seen with me?"

"Never." His grin turned mischievous. "I'm actually looking forward to spending more time with you, and I'm hoping you let me participate in your next adventure."

"I can't predict the future and have no idea if my friends and I will be doing any more sleuthing that doesn't involve a flat-screen television." When his smile faded into a pout, I pressed a gentle kiss to his cheek. "But if we do, you'll be the first person I call."

ABOUT THE AUTHOR

Nola Robertson grew up in the Midwest and eventually migrated to a rural town in New Mexico, where she lives with her husband and three cats, all with unique personalities and a lot of attitude.

Though she started her author career writing paranormal and sci-fi romance, it didn't take long for her love of solving mysteries to have her writing cozies. When she's not busy working on her next DIY project or reading, she's plotting her next mystery adventure.